Secret Service Mandate 7266, otherwise known as the Ogmios Directive, sanctioned the formation of an elite team under the command of Sir Charles Wyndham. Their orders are to do anything and everything necessary to preserve the sovereignty of the British Isles. What that actually means is difficult to pin down. They are deniable. They act outside the law, removed from the security of the State.

If something went wrong they were on their own.

If something went right no one ever said thank you.

It was enough that when things went to hell, they were there. Sir Charles, known affectionately to his people as the old man, calls them the Forge Team, but their nickname amongst themselves is the Lost Cause.

They serve at the pleasure of Her Majesty and report to a faceless bureaucrat in the upper echelons of government known only as Control, though no one with the power to would ever admit that.

These five men and women are often the last hope.

ONE

"You have three minutes to live."

The voice was too loud in his earbud, but he didn't dare take it out. He wasn't trained for this. He wasn't *ready*.

"Choose quickly. Which of you is more valuable to me?"

The bomb vest was fairly standard. Given enough time, the right tools and maybe an online instructional video, Jude Lethe knew he could defuse it. No problem at all. Theoretically this was his thing. Practically? Ronan, Noah, Konstantin, Orla, any one of them stood a better chance of making it out of this in one piece than he did. He didn't have a computer. The closest he had to tools were his bare hands. And only one of those was free. The other clutched a dead man's switch so tightly his knuckles blanched white.

Professor Flynn stood next to him. She wore an identical jacket and squeezed a dead man's switch of her own.

"Just go. Run. Leave me," Flynn cried. Tears of defeat tracked down her face.

He shook his head. "If I run, both our vests go off." Lethe turned in a circle, shuffling his feet in place. The dizzying sight of dozens of police officers aiming their automatics at him did fuck all for his concentration.

"It's not what it looks like," he called out, trying to show them the switch without opening his hand. "Seriously. Don't do anything I'm going to regret, okay? We're not the bad guys here. The last thing we want to do is hurt anyone, least of all us."

Maybe they didn't speak English.

They didn't lower their guns.

A television news crew filmed them from behind the ring of police, so at least the folks back home would get to see him go out in a blaze of glory. The rest of the *Plaza de Armas* was emptying out fast. More officers cleared the gawking tourists with their camera phones; the modern world was shit, Lethe decided, full of voyeurs happy to snap away until they got the perfect picture of the suicide bombers.

Well, fuck that for a game of soldiers. Lethe had no intention of becoming a crime statistic.

The brightly coloured tee-shirts and short sleeved shirts of the Cathedral's visitors added colour to the square as they evacuated the centuries-old building. They fanned out into two streams, rushing down the steps either side of the bombers.

"Tick tock, Mr Lethe."

The officers screamed something. The words were unintelligible. Even if he'd spoken rudimentary Spanish he wouldn't have been able to untangle them. Not knowing what they meant made them easy to ignore.

He should take Flynn at her word, he knew, run, leave her to burn.

He was more valuable.

But he wasn't going to do that, even if it was the logical choice. It wasn't him. And maybe he was wrong. Maybe *his* vest was the live one.

Maybe they both were.

He stared into Flynn's terrified eyes, and knew she saw fear in his.

She took the choice of out his hands.

"Go!" she said.

TWO

Ten days earlier

Jude Lethe wasn't a natural traveller.

The flight had been a bitch, and he'd let the man in the seat beside him know all about just how uncomfortable the cramped seats were, every strain of germ filling the recycled air and the reconstituted nature of the so-called potato in the airline food. He couldn't help himself. He knew it was annoying, eleven on a scale of ten, but he kept talking anyway. It wasn't about the flight. It was about the old man. He felt *betrayed*. It was a strong word, but that was just how pissed off he was to be out here. He didn't do field work. That wasn't his role in the team. He was the puppet master. He saw the big picture. He directed the show. What he didn't do was get his hands dirty.

Yet here he was, dragging a suitcase through Lima airport instead of back in The Nest, the nerve centre of the team's entire operation. He wasn't sure why he was supposed to care about some archaeological dig in the arse end of nowhere, or the technical specialist he was supposed to be relieving. All he could think was that this professor woman must be pretty important to warrant Sir Charles Wyndham sending him out here to run a couple of industrial ground scanners because someone thought they'd found a lost city buried beneath a bloody mountain. It sounded less like James Bond to Lethe and more like Bear Grylls's *Man Vs Wild*, though Lethe was damned if he was going to drink his own piss.

"I shouldn't be here," Lethe said as he trailed behind Noah Larkin. "You know that. I know that. This is stupid. I should be back at Nonesuch."

"You're such a fanny," Noah chuckled. At least *someone* was having fun. "The old man wouldn't send you if he thought you'd be in any danger, would he? I mean he likes you, even if he's not so keen on me."

"I'm never part of the shit show, that's your job. *This* isn't what I do," Lethe knew he'd already made the point half a dozen times during the flight, but he couldn't help himself. He was stuck on repeat. "You know why it's true? Because I'm not damaged like everyone else in this damned team."

"If you say so."

"Seriously, mate. Get me back in one piece."

"Read you loud and clear, Inspector Gadget."

Lethe decided to let that one go.

"I mean what are we even walking into? The old man gets a 'Help Me, Obi-Wan' call from some woman he no doubt did the dirty with a billion years ago, and his first thought is, 'I know, let's send poor old Mister Lethe out into the middle of the Peruvian jungle.'" Lethe paused. "You're not listening to me, are you?"

"Nope."

"You're a bastard, aren't you?"

"Yep."

"What I want to know is why you point blank refuse to tell me what happened to her old tech guy?"

Noah turned around. "You really want to know?"

"Zigazig ah."

"You're such a nerd. Fine. You really want to know. I'll tell you. But you're not going to like it."

"I knew that much when you wouldn't tell me. So?"

"He was kidnapped."

"Kidnapped? Seriously?" Lethe couldn't help himself; that came out much louder than he'd intended.

If looks could have killed, he'd have been six feet under. Noah stared him down.

"Three members of an archaeological survey team were snatched four days ago. Nobody's heard from them since."

"Who took them?"

"Your guess is as good as mine."

"I don't like this."

"You don't have to."

"Okay. One question: what's to stop *me* from getting kidnapped too?"

Noah smiled.

"I'd have thought that was obvious. Me."

THREE

Professor Camila Morais was in her fifties, though looked a decade younger, easily. She was a striking woman with delicate features and close-cropped curly black hair. And if she'd realised he was judging her by her appearance she would probably have torn Lethe a new one. He shook her hand, noting the hard callouses that spoke of decades working on digs.

She welcomed them with a generous smile, and flawless English.

Lethe was a little taken aback. He wasn't sure quite what he had expected, a female version of the old man, maybe? He wasn't comfortable around women at the best of times, and certainly not when they were as intimidatingly beautiful as Morais.

He looked anywhere but at her, a fact that Noah didn't miss. As Morais led them from the arrivals gate, he leaned in close to Lethe and whispered, "She's old enough to be your mum, you bad lad."

"Shut up, you prick," Lethe said as they walked out through the doors.

Morais waited for them on the other side, "I can't tell you how grateful I am that you came. I know we are small potatoes compared with what you usually do, but we really need your help."

"This is what we do," Lethe said. It was a half-truth as opposed to an outright lie.

It took several minutes to get to the car park. It was hotter than hell. Halfway there and he found himself longing for the air-conditioning of the damned plane with the kind of fondness best reserved for half-forgotten lovers, the sweat clinging to the back of his shirt. Morais drove a compact Toyota. Best guess, a rental. It was the newest car in the lot. No way did archaeology pay that well.

As they wove between the parked cars a motorbike, moving far too fast for such a crowded space, veered out of Lethe's way, still close enough for the rider to come away with a good idea of his religion.

"Fond of life, arsehole?" Lethe yelled after the man.

Morais smiled at him across the roof of her car. "I take it you haven't been to this delightful land before, Mr Lethe?"

"That obvious?" he replied, climbing into the back. The seats were leather. They were hot enough to fry an egg on.

Noah rode shotgun.

"Well, hold on tight," she said with a grin.

Lethe reached for his seatbelt.

There wasn't one.

Negotiating the car park was an experience he wouldn't forget in a hurry. There was order to the process; cars pushed their way toward the main road, vying for space aggressively. Nobody gave an inch. They forced their way through the jam of traffic miraculously without colliding. It only got worse outside the airport.

Morais floored the accelerator, losing them in a sea of traffic and a rage of horns. A light ahead turned red and, at the last possible second, she slammed on the brakes, bringing them to a screeching halt. Every car around them did the same.

The beaten up taxi cab on Lethe's right crossed over into their lane. The white lines were more of a suggestion than a rule.

Another set of lights and another dizzyingly abrupt halt.

The brakes of the ancient Beetle in front of them were so shrill they would have pierced his eardrums without the layer of glass between them. The Beetle's brake pads had long since waved the white flag.

Morais took a short cut through a residential area without indicating. All the houses along the strip were unfinished. Piles of bricks and construction dust were everywhere. Many houses were three or four storeys, but none of them were complete. Metal rebar thrust up into the sky. None of the buildings had the sloping roofs he was used to in Britain, instead they had an open-air upper floor. His first thought was that the owners were ready to throw up another level should a batch of bricks fall off the back of a lorry, but that wasn't it, it was all about taxes. Unfinished building projects didn't need to pay off the government.

Lethe's attention returned to the road.

Morais leant on her horn as she raced headlong towards a blind intersection. Houses blocked her view of oncoming traffic from the crossing street.

She blasted through.

"You okay back there, Judy?" Noah asked him.

"Just peachy, thanks," Lethe replied.

Morais swerved the car back onto the major road without signalling, shifting lanes until they'd crossed over to the far right. Another road merged with their lane. A 90s Civic rattled along the potholed slip road, inching closer and closer to collision as the roads converged. A terrified *gringo* stared across at him. They drew closer like star-crossed lovers in the night, until Lethe could see the blood vessels in the whites of the man's eyes.

At the last possible second the Civic dropped back.

Lethe closed his eyes.

Morais, on the other hand, chatted away happily with Noah in the front. He concentrated on what she had to say; it was that or keep his eyes on the road, and that way lay madness.

"My people are prisoners, Noah. I need you to find them. I don't know who has them. I don't even know if they're still in Lima."

"I stay with Jude," Noah insisted. "Sir Charles was *very* clear on that. We're a package. And as much as I appreciate you must be worried about your friends, we didn't come here to find anyone. Pretty boy is here to work his magic with some arcane machine, then we're out of here. That was the deal you made with the old man."

"And if I were to appeal to your better nature?"

"I don't have one."

She laughed at that. "I'm sure that's true. I can pay you if you prefer?"

"I'm not leaving Jude in the middle of nowhere to fend for himself. He can barely tie his own shoes."

"I can hear you, you know," Lethe put in from the back seat.

"I promise you, he'll be quite safe. After what happened I've hired protection. The dig is secure."

Noah pondered this for a moment.

"How much?"

"Noah!" Lethe cut across their negotiation.

"It's okay, I wasn't serious. You and me, kiddo. I stay with you. But *if* I think it's kosher, I'll look for their people, okay?"

"You aren't leaving me."

"Did I say I was? If anything fails the sniff test we're out of here, you have my word."

Morais sighed and said, "Please, just don't wait until they're dead."

"Can I ask you something?"

"I don't have anything to hide," she said.

"Why not go to the police?" It was a good question. Noah had a habit of cutting through the bullshit and getting right to the heart of the matter. In this case, the authorities were better positioned for a man hunt.

"Because I'm here illegally. My visa was refused. There are dozens of organizations smuggling exotic animals into this country every day. There's a huge market for it. Most of that money gets funnelled back into local terrorism. Pay enough cold hard cash and the smugglers will take people over. It's not so different."

"And these local terrorists are behind the kidnap of your friends?" Noah asked.

"The Shining Path? It's likely, yes."

"Shining Path? I thought they were history?"

Morais didn't reply.

"Did you all come over together, or were the others here legitimately?" Lethe did his best to ignore the near fatality up ahead as a motorcyclist barely avoided going beneath a truck.

"They're American, that blue passport helps. My visa was refused because I asked for permission to dig near Macchu Picchu. I told my colleagues to say they were teaching at Lima's university. The difference was enough."

The car dipped into a pothole the size of a small military junta. The side of Lethe's head hammered off the roof. Morais didn't apologise. He saw her smile in the rear view mirror and knew she was giving him the full tourist experience. Another horn blared. Lethe glanced back to see the battered and rusty grille of a huge transport lorry filling the rear window. There was nothing else. Just the grille. Morais swerved the car into the next lane, letting the lorry pass. More horns. At the next set of lights, another car somehow squeezed into the tiny gap between them. It was dizzying. The driver, a young man with a car full of friends, leant out of the window and yelled insults or imprecations at Morais. She ignored him. The lights changed and the other car roared off, choking out a thick cloud of black exhaust fumes in its wake.

Dusk fell as they reached the city limits.

The road ahead was rougher still. There were no streetlights to light the way. The traffic thinned out as the buildings with bars on the windows and walls graphitised with angry political slogans and crude caricatures gave way to dusty hills dotted with slum housing.

An hour later they stopped at a roadside diner with too-bright strip lighting and literal greasy spoons to grab a bite to eat, then drove on.

Lethe settled down in the back to get some sleep.

FOUR

Lethe hated it here.

He didn't have anything against Peru in particular, apart from the dust and the dirt and the language and the general stench of poverty that wormed its way into everything. Morais was fluent in Spanish as well as English and her native Portuguese. Noah knew enough words to get by, though his vocabulary was probably better suited to a brothel than an archaeological dig. Lethe felt left out. He wasn't good at being the odd one out. But he was lying to himself, too. It wasn't about this place. He could have been anywhere in the world and he'd still want to be back at Nonesuch. That was home. The Nest was where he made a difference. Not out here.

He couldn't understand why the old man had taken such a huge risk in pulling him out of his comfort zone and sticking him in this hell hole. It didn't make sense. And Lethe didn't like it when things didn't make sense.

The tourist train rolled through the town centre of Aguas Calientes. Quite literally through the centre, as the railway line ran the length of what should have been the main street. Morais explained that there were no roads into this town. The only way in was by train. So shops and restaurants had built up around the railway. For most people, Aguas Calientes served as a base from which to visit the Inca city of Machu Picchu. It consisted of two streets, one of which followed the tracks and another that formed a narrow walking trail up what looked like an impossibly steep hill. The only others vehicles here were either slick tourist buses taking their passengers up to the ruins and back, or a few bikes.

After disembarking, Morais led them to a rather basic looking hotel where they met the survey team.

Lethe wasn't good with names. They went around the circle introducing themselves and he'd forgotten every one of them before he heard the next. There was one woman, American (or perhaps Canadian, he couldn't tell the difference) with the dusty blonde hair, who made the thought of spending a few days halfway up a mountain almost bearable.

Lethe turned down the offer of food and instead opted for coca tea to help with his altitude sickness. Noah seemed happy enough to mix with the crew, but Lethe gave his excuses and retreated up to his room. Noah came by to check on him an hour later, but he needn't have bothered. He was fine. The room was simple: sparse furniture and a bed with clean sheets. There was no television, no telephone, no trouser press, and more frustratingly, no Wi-Fi. "Go have fun," Lethe told him. "It's not like I can get into any trouble up here."

"You sure?"

He nodded. "I need to sleep."

"Whatever you say, boss."

After Noah left he lay on the bed fully dressed and stared up at the cracks in the ceiling. It felt as though he'd been travelling for decades—and landed somewhere back around 1830. He really didn't like being so disconnected from the world. He very nearly booted up his laptop and satellite modem just to browse the front pages of a couple of newspapers back home so he could fool himself into thinking everything was normal, but he closed his eyes instead.

FIVE

The vintage bus had no shock absorbers left. They lurched up the mountain road, juddering from side to side, and veering perilously close to the edge. Lethe could have done without breakfast. Live and learn. It was a gruelling two-hour drive up a dizzying gradient on a cracked and broken road riddled with potholes. A loose chunk of road broke free and tumbled down the side of the mountain, offering a glimpse of their fate if the driver lost his concentration. More of the road crumbled beneath their wheels. Lethe offered a prayer to whatever god looked out for stupid travellers who should have stayed at home. It was better not to look out of the window, he decided, choosing ignorance. He didn't want to think about the sheer drop just a metre or two away from the worn-smooth tyres. The driver did this journey every day, he told himself over and over, willing the mantra to weave a spell around the old bus.

They didn't plummet to their deaths.

"Better hold on," the driver, whose name was Guilherme, called back to his passengers. "The road ahead gets a little rough."

Lethe tried not to laugh at the thought of this being the smooth. Nobody else found it funny. He tightened his grip on the seat in front of him. He definitely shouldn't have had breakfast.

Guilherme was right. The road was even rougher now, but on the bright side no one else was crazy enough to be coming the other way. They came to what looked for all the world like a dead end. A couple of the passengers disembarked, working quickly in the blistering heat to clear the foliage that obscured the path's continued rise toward the summit. The road was a mess. Decay had sunk hungry teeth into it. He couldn't believe it was still traversable, even by a modern off-road four by four, never mind a rickety old bus. They followed the road up the side of a mountain. With each twist and turn the surface deteriorated further. The bus's chassis creaked and groaned as the wheels dropped into deep craters and juddered out the other side.

As well as his laptop and satellite modem, Lethe carried the operator's manual for the Ground Penetrating Radar and back-up copies of the associated software. It was impossible to focus on the words so he didn't bother trying to read. It wasn't like he needed the manual anyway. He was one with the machine and the machine was one with him. Or something like that.

Guilherme doubled up as the hardware specialist. He'd be setting up the radar equipment. An older Peruvian woman, Beatriz, wore a scarf on her head. She was not so slowly driving Noah insane with her incessant babble of family, dogs, hobbies and just about everything else. Or at least that's what he assumed, given every word was in Spanish. Could have been sharing the nuclear codes for all he knew. He didn't envy Noah.

Behind him sat Morais and her assistant, Cathy, who it turned out was a Canadian archaeology student. Lethe tried not to look at her, because he felt like a creep every time he did; especially as the first thing he looked for was a ring. Even if there was a boyfriend back home, Canada was a long way away. He was lying to himself, of course. He'd barely managed three awkward words to her. What he could tell was that she was nervous about something. Hardly surprising with four armed men occupying the back seats of the bus.

Lethe hadn't caught their names and didn't much care. It wasn't the guns, there was just something about them that didn't sit right, but Noah seemed okay with them. There was no getting around the fact they were eerily quiet, though. They nursed their automatic weapons in silence, staring out of the windows as the bus bumped and lurched. They were Morais's hired muscle. Before they'd set off that morning she'd tried to set their mind at ease, her logic that no one would come after them because they weren't as valuable as three scientists from Yale. That didn't do anything for Lethe's ego, or his peace of mind. Noah glanced in their direction a couple of times, he realised, so maybe he wasn't cool with them after all. Then again, outside of Frosty, Koni and Orla who did Noah trust?

It was mid-morning by the time they finally arrived at the dig site, a wide plateau more than half way up the mountainside.

On the far side of the relatively flat ground, the rock face continued to a distant peak high above them. On the near side, close to the road, the ground simply dropped away into nothing. Lethe's legs were unsteady as he stepped off the bus. The four mercenaries fanned out and climbed to higher ground, taking up positions while the rest of the passengers unloaded equipment. Lethe walked over to the edge, getting as close as he dared. There was no safety barrier to prevent him pitching over into oblivion, and no warning signs to state the obvious, either. This wasn't exactly a tourist trap, but the view was breath-taking. It was like staring at the Dales through a magnifying glass. The sacred valley wound its way between a series of great peaks, mostly covered in greenery but for occasional rocky breaks. The tops of each mountain merged with wispy clouds. Brilliant sunshine rendered the whole scene almost hyper-real, like some intense acid trip.

In the distance, Lethe saw what must have been Machu Picchu.

He couldn't make out much detail, but the series of man-made walls were obvious even from here. It was as though someone had carved a giant staircase into the side of the mountain.

Reluctantly, he turned his back on the stunning vista and went to help Guilherme with the GPR equipment.

He could see only two of the mercs, now.

One stood at the top of the road, keeping an eye out for vehicles. The other was a couple of hundred yards above them, standing on a rocky outcrop smoking a cigarette.

Their presence wasn't particularly reassuring.

Noah carried equipment from the bus, but his eyes were scanning the terrain. Lethe tried to think like him: a single exit wasn't ideal. It was far too easy to cut them off if someone wanted to. Escape upwards was a possibility, but only on foot. But how high could he climb, realistically, before he took a bullet in the spine? Everything was so exposed.

One small blessing though; it wasn't so unbearably hot up here in the mountains that he thought he was going to melt.

Under Morais's direction, Guilherme and Cathy set up the radar equipment near the cliff face. Noah and Lethe set up a small table and chairs nearby, while Beatriz busied herself with building a camp fire and prepping lunch.

Once the table was up, Lethe took his laptop and the miniature satellite dish from his case. It took him a couple minutes to get a signal but it wasn't long before a flood of emails landed in his inbox. Lethe plugged in his mobile into the USB port to charge it while he read through his messages. Noah worked on starting the portable generator.

Lunch was a simple but filling meal of chicken, rice and beans. It didn't taste of particularly anything, but beggars couldn't be choosers.

Afterwards, they finished setting up the first of the Ground Penetrating Radar units. He wanted to install the software on his own machine, but instead they gave him a dinosaur in processor terms which already had the necessary software loaded. The interface was quite simple, though not necessarily the most efficient design. They had five scanners to configure. What Lethe couldn't work out, looking at the rig now, was why they had dragged him to the bottom of the planet to help when any half decent computer studies student could have learned the system in a morning. Guilherme it turned out, had never used the equipment outside of a controlled environment, so there was an element of fake-it or make-it-up with the finer calibrations, which was only confused by random interference. It took them ages to work out cell phone signals were interfering with the readings. Once everyone killed their phones and Lethe disabled the satellite modem, the readings settled down.

A shrill whistle from one of the mercenaries interrupted Lethe's concentration. Morais hustled the small team under cover. Lethe grabbed his own laptop, abandoning the crappy old one, and ran after the others. They took shelter beneath a large rock that jutted out from the cliff. Morais checked they were okay, and then surprised Lethe by drawing a gun. "Stay here," she said, and rushed off towards the road.

Then the gunfire started.

Oh shit, oh shit. Lethe tried not to panic. The others were surprisingly calm, even Beatriz stood ready. She wielded a wooden spoon like a weapon.

Lethe was used to gunfire, but it was usually filtered through his comms link. This was considerably more *brutal*. Seconds later, Noah ghosted past their position, moving fast, body low, gun close to the ground.

A bullet ricocheted from the rock above Lethe's head.

The familiar sound of Noah's answering fire came in a quick burst; three shots. More automatic fire. Another bullet punched a hole in the rock wall uncomfortably close to his head. Instinct screamed to break cover and run for the bus. Instinct was stupid. Moving would get them killed. He kept his head down.

More yelling and more gunfire, then silence.

And the silence was so much worse than all of the shots combined.

He looked at the others. They seemed eerily calm, all things considered.

Lethe's bones all but jumped out of his skin as Morais appeared suddenly. "All clear. You guys can come out now."

Lethe and the others clambered slowly from their hiding places. Noah ran back to them.

"You okay?" he asked Lethe, ignoring the others.

He nodded. "Fine. What happened?"

Noah rounded on Morais. He looked pissed.

"Yeah, time to do some explaining, Prof?"

"*El Sendero Luminoso,*" Morais said, as though that explained everything.

"The Shining Path?"

She nodded.

"Wearing police uniforms?"

"They do that a lot."

"Your men fired first. How do you know they weren't real police?"

"Oh, they *were* real police. But that doesn't change their allegiances. Most departments in this region are controlled by the Shining Path. They want our equipment and supplies, it's worth cash. So are we. Hence the kidnappings."

"Fuck me, what the hell has the old man got us into here?"

"They must have followed us from town. Or maybe we didn't hide the trail well enough. Either way this wasn't about an expired visa."

She had a point; if the police planned to arrest Morais for being in the country illegally, they'd come for her at the hotel. They wouldn't come out to the mountain. This was an ambush.

Noah stared at the road rather than at Morais. He was bringing his temper under control.

"Next time," he said coldly, "You warn us when we're walking into the line of fire. Once, I'll forgive, but not twice."

"My apologies, Mister Larkin," Morais said with a smile. "Charles led me to believe you were familiar with the situation inside the region. Everyone knows the police here are loyal to terrorists. *Outside* of the region, the government likes to keep it quiet, but the reality is they have lost control of a huge chunk of the country."

Noah actually growled.

Lethe had seen him this angry before. People had a habit of dying when he lost his shit. He was like the Incredible Hulk without the green skin, the muscles or the purple trousers. "Stand down, Noah," he said quietly, so it didn't sound like an order. It took half a minute before Noah managed to rein in his temper. Even then, it was obvious he wasn't happy.

One of the mercenaries approached. Blood covered one side of his face. He held a hand to his head. He said something in Spanish and Beatriz went to help him.

"What did he say?" Lethe asked. He didn't like the sight of blood.

"The road's clear," Morais replied.

"The blood?"

"A bullet caught his ear."

"He got lucky," Noah said. "If it had been me I wouldn't have pierced his ear."

"I speak English," the merc grunted.

"Good," Noah said, and walked away.

Morais directed two of the uninjured mercs to dispose of the bodies of their attackers. They moved off without a word. Meanwhile, Beatriz had opened the first aid kit and was attempting to staunch the first merc's bleeding ear.

Lethe watched as the two men stripped the dead officers of their clothes and weapons with practiced efficiency. There were four bodies. It didn't take them long to get them down to their underwear. Then they dragged the bodies to the edge of the road and kicked them over the precipice without a second thought.

"We got lucky," Noah said, "Approaching from below they were at a disadvantage. If they'd been bedded in above, we'd be fucked. This place is a nightmare. A bit of luck and we'd have had nowhere to go."

"Just like shooting wamp rats back home in Beggar's Canyon," Lethe said.

"You're a strange man."

"Something about this whole thing stinks," Lethe said.

"It does. But don't say a word. Not here. Too many unknowns."

Lethe nodded. They were on the same page.

An engine started and tyres rumbled on the road. Lethe saw a police car move into sight. One of the mercs drove it up onto the plateau.

Morais joined them. "The police in Aguas Calientes have two vehicles."

"One now," Noah said.

"Indeed. Which means we've neutralised half of our enemy's resources. So thank you. You've helped buy us a chance."

"I wasn't helping you. I was looking after pretty boy here."

"Same thing in this instance."

"Not really." He looked at the woman. There was something in the way he narrowed his gaze, trying to see a truth written on her face, that suggested there was something here he wasn't buying. "Can I ask you a question, Professor?"

"Camila."

"I'll stick with Prof, thanks. So, tell me, why are you doing this? Because I don't get it. Four of your team have been kidnapped, now you've been attacked by the local law, and here's the curious thing, I don't see anyone packing up to go. It doesn't make a blind bit of sense to me, to be honest."

Morais's demeanour shifted; it was subtle but gone was the apologetic academic and in her place was her defiant twin. "We *have* to find the city," she insisted.

"Don't tell me, there are treasures beyond my wildest dreams buried beneath the mountain?"

"Millions of dollars' worth," she said.

"Marvellous. But you know what, that's still not worth getting yourself killed over."

"You don't understand, Mister Larkin. We need that money. It is the only way we can pay the ransom the Shining Path will demand for our people."

"And in the process fund the terrorists. It's not a good idea."

"It's better than leaving them to rot. They aren't soldiers. They are my friends."

"Who's to say they're not dead already?"

"That's not how the Shining Path do things. It's all about the money."

"Fine. It's still stupid. We need to go. Like you said, they're not soldiers. That means they'll have caved as soon as their captors put pressure on them. We're not safe here."

"If we don't find the city first, they will, and then we've got nothing to bring our people home and they've still got the money."

"That's not sound logic, Prof. Look, I don't mean to come off like a prick, but you're not thinking straight. What's to say your friends aren't in on it? People do strange things when it comes to vast sums of money."

She shook her head. "I can't let myself think like that. They are good people. I need to bring them home."

"Fine," Noah said again. "But that answers one question at least."

"Which is?"

"They'll be back, simple as that," Noah said, nodding at the trail below. "No way I'm leaving pretty boy up here alone. And before you say 'But my men will keep him safe' I don't care. I don't trust men who kill for money. Never have. Never will. The fact that their loyalty can be bought once means their loyalty can be bought twice."

"I understand," Morais replied. "I don't like it, but I understand."

SIX

Lethe spent an uncomfortable evening on the side of the mountain. It was surprisingly cold once the sun went down. Beatriz filled their bellies with a stew that was pretty tasty, and hot enough to stave off the chill.

The plan had been to return to the hotel before dark, but calibrating the GPR units took longer than expected. The multiple scanners added a surprising amount of complexity to the relatively simple process of setting up a single machine. Still not enough to warrant his presence, but maybe this wasn't beneath his talents after all. Long after darkness fell, with the mercenaries taking shifts to watch the road, and Beatriz and Cathy had turned in, Lethe and Guilherme kept on working. He didn't know where Noah was. Morais dozed in a deck chair.

The problem, he realised was that several of the radar units were incomplete. Some of the components had been damaged in transit, others lost, meaning they had to jerry rig them with substitute parts, which worked, in theory, but meant the machines weren't compatible with the software used to control them. This made Lethe's task one of improvisation. He had to decompile code and rewrite it to bring the radar online. It was the first interesting part of the entire trip, but nothing he couldn't have done remotely from Nonesuch. The raw radar images were grey with wavy black lines. Lethe wasn't sure how anyone could interpret anything meaningful from them. The magic happened when he ran the 3-D processor to combine multiple images into a single snapshot of what was within the rock. Even his untrained eye would have been able to make out any out-of-place formations within the cliff face.

"Wouldn't it just be easier to shift everything back to the hotel, get it working first, find a big rock to scan to make sure it all works, then come back here instead of freezing our arses off on the side of a mountain in the pitch dark?" Noah asked, circling around from his patrol.

"But not half as much fun, so stop complaining," Lethe said, not looking up. The scanners had detected an anomaly buried deep within the rock, and that was what he was using to calibrate the scanners.

"Suit yourself, but don't come running to me when you get a runny nose."

Over the next couple of hours he adjusted and refined the equipment, each time trying to improve the sharpness of the picture coming through from the imager. The problem was to penetrate the dense rock face he had no choice but to lower the frequency of the radar scans. The lower the frequency, the poorer the resolution of the image. And that was the contradiction he was juggling with.

"I'm a fucking genius," he said, then, loud enough to wake Morais. He heard the crunch of stones under feet as Noah and Guilherme came running. He grinned like an idiot as he leaned back so they could see the screen. "This is the part where you tremble in awe of my genius."

"If I knew what was so impressive I'm sure I would," Noah said.

"See that dark space there," he pointed. "That's our *eureka* moment," Lethe said, "A man-made chamber in the heart of the mountain. Meaning the Prof was on the money. There's gold in them there hills."

"Or at least a cave," Noah said.

This time it was Morais who put him straight, "No, your friend is quite right. The walls are too regular, for one thing," she explained. "Even under great pressure stone doesn't sheer like that, at least not in this region. That means what we're looking at is a man-made chamber."

"Exactly," Lethe agreed, actually feeling jubilant. "Like I said, tremble in the presence of my magnificence. Been here a day, found the lost treasure. And I'm the one who's meant to stay at home."

Cathy came up beside Morais. She was wrapped in a blanket, and looked less than thrilled to be awake in the middle of the night.

"How can you be sure it's where the treasure's hidden?"

"I need to fix the resolution and fine tune the image a bit so we can be sure what we're looking at, but there's something in there."

"Then I guess it was worth interrupting my sleep," Cathy told him, with a slight smile, before she turned and walked away. "Goodnight, Mr Lethe," she called over her shoulder.

"It's Jude," he said.

"Looks like you've made yourself a new friend," Noah said, like a proud parent. At least he didn't ruffle his hair.

SEVEN

Lethe woke with a sore back and a sorer mood.

He'd never been a fan of camping, which was just a fancy way of sleeping rough as far as he was concerned, and the bone-deep chill in his muscles did nothing to change his mind. He unzipped the bag, emerging from the cocoon, stood and stretched. He ran his hands through his unkempt hair. It had been four days since he'd shaved. The stubble was annoyingly uneven and itched like a bastard. He looked around for the others.

The first thing he noticed was the open-topped jeep parked next to the bus and the police car. There were two armed men he didn't recognise beside it. Guilherme was talking to them, which he hoped meant he hadn't slept through the bad guys taking over the camp in the middle of the night.

Noah and Morais were deep in conversation next to the table. It was an animated exchange. Lethe hung back to eavesdrop when it became evident neither one of them had noticed him.

"I told you, not a prayer. I'm not leaving him. You can ask me a thousand times. You'll get the same answer a thousand and one times. I go where he goes."

"I've made arrangements for more men to guard him."

"He only needs one. Me. I gave the old man my word I'd get him back in one piece. I don't care if you're secretly the old man's mother-in-law. He's the boss, I do what he says. Nothing personal. I just don't trust you."

"Which is of course entirely personal," she objected. "But I know where my people are being held –"

"No you don't. You *think* you know, that's a fuck of a difference when it comes to a Search and Rescue, believe me," Noah cut across her. "And you don't even have an *address*. You have a district. *Barrios Altos* is a big place. We can't exactly go door to fucking door, woman. So again, I repeat. No."

"Fine. You're right. The people I hired to find the hostages might not be as skilled as you, but they assure me their intel is good. At the very worst it's a place to start looking. But you, if you were the one looking, I know you could do a lot better."

"Flattery ain't gonna cut it, Prof. I don't exactly blend in. The locals won't talk to me."

"Then take Carlos with you." Morais nodded towards the mercenary Beatriz had bandaged up. "He grew up in the *Barrios*, he knows the people. Let him help you."

Noah stared at the young man, who stood at the edge of the plateau overlooking the road, his assault rifle held ready.

"He makes a decent target," Noah said.

"Then it's settled." Morais turned to go.

"You really don't like being told no, do you?"

"No. I will reach out to Charles if it makes it easier for you? And good morning to you, Mr Lethe."

"Oh," Jude said, realising he'd been busted. He stepped out of the shadows with a rueful smile. "Good morning."

"I will make the call," Morais said, leaving Lethe alone with Noah.

"You can't seriously be considering leaving me here."

Noah scratched the side of his nose. "Honestly? No. Not really. I want to talk to the old man because there's stuff going on here that doesn't pass the sniff test. I want to know what he knows. And if that means playing along a bit, so be it. How long do you think this survey will take?"

Lethe shrugged, then exhaled through pursed lips. "A while. There's a lot of ground, er, wall to cover. We have to use the GPR to photograph the entire rock face, and that only tells us what's inside, not how to get to it. I'm assuming there's some kind of entrance, but where is anyone's guess. If we can't find one, it's a case of looking for a weak point in the chamber wall and blowing our way inside with controlled explosions—and praying to whatever the local gods are that we don't damage whatever's inside. There's nothing to say the entrance hasn't caved in years ago. It could be hidden up there," he indicated the outcrops above their heads. "Or down there," meaning over the edge of the staggering drop. "In which case we're talking much longer."

"So, in answer to my question...?"

"We could strike lucky today, or next week. Even the week after. But believe me, I don't want to stay here any longer than I have to."

"Right there with you. Of course, another way of looking at it is: the sooner those hostages come home, the sooner you and I can go home."

Noah had a point. It wasn't a point Lethe particularly appreciated, though.

"Can't you just get the old man to send Koni after them? Or Frosty maybe?"

"Faster for me."

"Look, don't make me beg, mate. I really don't want to be alone here. Please. And not to be a shit, but you said it was you and me, not you buggering off to play the hero and me all by my lonesome."

The problem was personality: Noah Larkin wasn't the kind of guy to call in the cavalry. He was the last resort. And realistically, with him and Lethe in Peru it was unlikely the old man would send in reinforcements, especially with Orla out of contact. She had been in her legend for months now, deep under cover. He didn't even know where, only that she was in place and playing the long game.

Morais called them over. Using the satellite uplink she'd raised the old man on Skype.

He didn't look best pleased at being disturbed.

"What can I do for you, Mister Larkin?"

"We've got a situation."

"Which is why you were dispatched. To deal with the situation. Do whatever you have to do to wrap this up as quickly as possible. It looks as though I need to send Ronan and Konstantin to Poland, so I will need you back here, Mister Lethe as soon as humanly possible."

"I can make Jude redundant in three days or less," Noah said. "But to do that I need to return to Lima."

"Leaving me exposed," Lethe pointed out. The old man didn't look best pleased by the thought.

"He'll be well protected," Morais said behind them.

"She's hired a bunch of mercs to babysit," Noah said.

"Camilla, I want you to give Mister Lethe a complete list of your hired guns. Lethe, run a background check on everyone involved. If you aren't happy, any red flags, you are to abort the mission and return home. Otherwise, Mister Larkin, you are cleared to go."

EIGHT

Lethe felt like Santa checking and double checking the names on Morais's list. They were all on there, everyone from Guilherme, Cathy and Beatriz to the hired guns. The uplink wasn't stable and time was limited, but there was no way he was sticking around without Noah to watch his back unless he knew exactly who he was working with. It took him a moment to remotely access the Nest and run a series of checks through national and international police records. For the sake of thoroughness he also ran the names through the CIA, NSA and FBI databases and Interpol. Those were the legitimate engines he trawled. He was more interested in the underground sites on the Sub Net he frequented.

The searches returned zero hits. No matches. No red flags. That was almost more worrying for soldiers of fortune. As far as he could tell, the four men had worked for a variety of security firms, mostly tasked with guarding installations like this. Nothing particularly heavy duty. Two of them were ex-police officers. Another pair had some significant run-ins with the law in their youth, but since then they'd been clean. He didn't turn up any links to the Shining Path or any other known terrorist organizations or sympathisers.

Like or not, they were clean—or so very, very dirty they were connected well enough to have someone sanitise their digital footprint—which was less likely. Reluctantly, he found Noah and told him, "Okay, looks like they're good."

"What about Carlos? Anything interesting?"

"Nothing. These guys are vanilla."

Noah stared at him. Lethe couldn't read him. After a couple of seconds Noah nodded, dismissing whatever doubts he had. He smiled.

"Then it's all good. You do your thing, I'll do mine, and we'll have you back at Nonesuch in no time."

Lethe was less convinced. He stood there, a sinking feeling in his gut, as he watched Noah and Carlos climb into the jeep.

The young merc gunned the engine.

"Good luck," Morais said. "And again, I know you're not doing this for me, but thank you."

"Your intel had better be good, Prof," Noah replied. He banged on the side of the jeep, signalling Carlos to floor it. The jeep spat up a cloud of dirt and dust as it roared away. A moment later it was out of sight and, a couple of minutes after that, out of earshot, too.

Lethe sighed.

At least the new crew had rolled in with fresh supplies: extra food and more blankets among them.

"Tamales?" It was Beatriz. She held up a pot and smiled at him.

"Oh God, yes. Feed me Seymour," Lethe grinned. He was absolutely famished. He took one of the savoury wraps and sank his teeth into the corn, boiled egg and chicken filling. The stuff dribbled down his chin. When he finally got back to England, he was going to have to look up the number of a Peruvian restaurant within delivery radius of Nonesuch.

Or perhaps he could ask the old man to install Beatriz as permanent chef. He took another bite without wiping his chin, and another until it was half gone, then crossed the plateau back to the bank of equipment.

He was getting the hang of this GPR. He'd already identified a potential weak point in the rock, where, if they had no other choice they could set the C4. There was a lot of rock face left, more than enough to hide a way in. He hoped.

He explained his findings to Morais, who couldn't hide her delight.

"There is one thing I find kinda odd," Lethe said to her.

"What's that?"

"Well, much to my own disgust I wound up checking the manual. There's a reference guide that basically identifies every kind of material you're likely to scan based on the pattern captured by the equipment. The walls are metal, I'm absolutely sure of it. Now, I'm no history buff, but I doubt the Inca used metal to build their walls."

Morais chuckled. "Quite right. The Inca were proficient with gold and copper, and had uses for metal beyond the symbolic, but they didn't build with it."

Lethe frowned. "So what am I seeing?"

"The Inca built walls with shaped stones, interlocked like jigsaw puzzles so they would stay up without any kind of cement. It's quite remarkable really. In fact, it's safe to say the Inca were a remarkable people, Mr Lethe."

Morais clapped him on the shoulder and moved off to help Guilherme move the radar equipment for the next survey. Lethe decided to take a break. He strolled over to the winding road and headed down. He wasn't looking for anything more than a change of scenery. One hundred metres down he came up against one of the hired guns. The man unshouldered his rifle as Lethe approached.

"*A dónde estás yendo?*" It sounded like a demand.

He didn't point the weapon directly at Lethe, but he waved it around animatedly enough that his meaning was clear.

"Woah!" Lethe held up both hands up, palms out. "Take it easy. No need to get excited. I'm just going for a walk. Okay? A walk?" He mimed walking with his fingers.

"*Vuelva ahi!*"

It could have been a yes, could have been a no, but Lethe read it more as an over-my-dead-body kind of response. He got the message as the man jabbed the muzzle back in the direction of the camp. He didn't argue. He trudged back up the road. Morais waited for him at the top.

"Ah, sorry about that," she said a little ruefully. "I should have warned you. Given everything that happened, I thought it best to make sure you didn't wander off. I don't want to have to explain to Mister Larkin why you got yourself killed. Somehow I don't think he'd be very forgiving."

"I understand," Lethe said, and he did, even if it left him feeling like a prisoner here. "I should get back to work anyway."

"Again, I am very sorry. Sometimes men like these forget their manners."

"I'm pretty sure he said 'please'," Lethe said.

The process of conducting the geological survey was by necessity meticulous and time consuming but, much like coding, it had the ability to suck you in. Lethe was losing himself in the minutia of the task, and it was strangely captivating. It was a good fit for the more obsessive aspect of his personality. And as the pattern began to reveal itself, every hint of wall defining the mysterious shape it hid, and every deeper scar that might just as easily be an artefact as a door, kept him staring, kept him searching, because quite simply he needed to know. It wasn't all that much different from digging into the corners of the Dark Net for critical information, unearthing clues, in enigmatic address references and following leads from hidden meeting place to another.

It was getting dark and he'd been working for four hours straight, which meant he was an hour late to check in with Noah.

He powered up the satellite modem. His phone beeped furiously with missed call alerts. He speed-dialled Noah.

"Where were you?"

"Busy." Lethe said.

"Where are you?"

"Back in Cusco. We're waiting for the flight. I'll give him this much, young Carlos here is *very* keen to get me to Lima. How's you?"

"All quiet. I've mapped more of the chamber walls inside the mountain. It's pretty big. No sign of the entrance yet, but there's at least one place we can blow if push comes to shove."

"Good. Keep me posted. And next time check in when you're supposed to. Otherwise I'll have to come back there and beat your arse, got it?"

"Sorry."

"No you're not. But I'm serious, Jude. I can't be worrying about you. Shit like that gets you killed in this game."

"I know."

Lethe killed the connection. Dinner was almost ready. It felt like all he was doing was working and eating, eating and working. He took a couple of minutes to fire off a brief Situation Report for the old man and caught up on some of his emails before joining the others.

"Smells good," he said, pulling up a seat.

This time Beatriz served up soup and a flatbread she called *pan chuta*.

To Lethe's surprise, Cathy took the seat beside him. "I saw your run-in with the prison guard," she said. "Are you okay?"

"I'm fine," Lethe replied. "But yeah I can't tell if they're here to protect us or keep us on lockdown."

"At least the food's good," she said with a grin. "Beatriz is a genius. She's promised me a load of recipes for when I fly out."

"You like cooking?"

"Oh dear god no. No, no and thrice no. My dad's a chef. I'll pass them on to him. He's always asking for new things to try."

"I don't suppose the Prof's mentioned anything about going back to the hotel? I could really do with a shower and please don't agree with that too quickly."

"I can ask. She's a bit single-minded when it comes to work. Tends to forget about the niceties, like hygiene. There's so many layers of dirt on me I could host a dig of my own." Lethe smiled at that.

Maybe travelling wasn't so bad after all.

NINE

Lethe awoke to shouting. The shock of it was jarring. He was immediately alert. Heart thundering.

Disorientated.

In the distance: the unmistakable sound of a helicopter approaching, blades *whumping* against the morning air. It was met by a flurry of activity in the camp.

Lethe clambered out of his sack and stood up, trying to swallow down the panic and not doing a very good job of it. Noah, or a gun, either one of them would have done right then. Or at a push Frosty could come parachuting in like some guardian ex-para angel. Or maybe not. He stashed his laptop in its metal case. As far as protection went, it wasn't much. He couldn't do much better though. Not in the sixty seconds or so he had to react. He had to think of himself. And that thought lasted about two seconds until he realised that he couldn't see Cathy.

It was chaos. The darkness lit up sporadically with bursts of gunfire. He could hear the spits of impact as the shells bit home. He tried to focus himself, picture the camp in his mind's eye, and orientate himself to the onslaught. He didn't trust himself to run, not when the sheer drop off the side of the plateau promised certain death. The problem was, not running meant becoming a sitting duck.

The helicopter swooped in. The spotlight from its underside strobed across the plateau, settling on two of the black-clad mercenaries as they ran into position. They returned fire as the ducked under cover.

Lethe couldn't move.

He was rooted to the spot, hypnotised by the searchlight.

"This way, Señor!"

It took him a moment to realise *Señor* was him. Beatriz waved frantically at him. The backlight from the torch in her hand transformed her into an ancient avenging god haunting the hills. Lethe ran towards the light, crouching low, arms and legs pumping furiously as he covered the ground fast. One of the mercenaries stepped into his path, machine gun raised, and loosed a volley of useless gunfire up into the sky. Lethe ducked around him, stumbling. He felt something, and suddenly he was soaked. He didn't dare slow by even a footstep.

He reached Beatriz.

She lay face down on the ground.

He thought for one sickening second that she'd been hit, but as he crouched beside her she looked up, and shining her light on him, gasped, "Oh my God. You are hit!"

But that didn't feel right.

He shook his head.

But in the torchlight it was obvious what had soaked him; blood covered his clothes, his hands, everything. Fighting down the urge to vomit, he shook his head.

"Not mine," he said, trying to reassure her, but he wasn't sure she believed him. She grabbed him by the bloody sleeve and dragged him to the far side of the bus. A ricochet came frighteningly close. More bullets struck the metal shell of the ancient vehicle, but at this angle the bus worked as a shield against the worst of the shooting. He saw Cathy crouched beside one of the big rubber wheels. She looked haunted. Not just frightened. Way beyond that. Terror gripped her. She'd found her own mortality on this mountain and wasn't coping with it. Lethe crouched down beside her. He wanted to reach out, to hold her, to tell her it'd be all right, but he didn't have it in him to lie.

The helicopter swept overhead, blades churning up the air around them as its searchlight strafed across the plateau. The downdraft kicked up an unholy dust storm, whipping debris into Lethe's eyes and mouth. A fresh hail of machine gun fire spat from above, the staccato rattle of bullets created a terrifying percussion as the shots tore into the side of the bus. Lethe saw the tail rotor light up with each fresh volley, and recognised the markings.

It was a police chopper.

A sudden flurry of movement across the plateau caught his eye: Morais running towards them. She moved awkwardly. It took him a second to realise why; she was carrying something. One of the GPR scanners? No. There was no way she'd managed to uncouple the array in the few seconds since the attack began. The silhouette was cylindrical. A pipe? "Over here," Lethe yelled, his voice swallowed by the battering wind.

She didn't hear him, or wasn't listening.

Morais stopped dead in her tracks.

She was directly in the line of fire.

He expected two things to happen in that moment: Morais to raise her hands in surrender, and the gunman to cut her down in a hail of bullets.

"What the fuck is she doing?" Lethe yelled uselessly. The woman dropped to one knee and swung the metal tube up over her shoulder. With that one motion he knew exactly what she was doing.

"Holy Mother of Christ," he breathed. With a flare of red, the heatseeker burst from the barrel of Morais's rocket launcher and hurtled with dizzying speed into the belly of the helicopter. Lethe shielded his eyes from the blinding explosion. Even so, the flames turned his flesh translucent, in that heartbeat it was bright enough for night to turn to day and every blood vessel and capillary in his hands to become visible. The noise was worse. The metal shrieked as it twisted, the crash sounding like thunder as the tortured wreck came down. It collided with the side of the mountain below the plateau and then rolled out of sight. Each impact faded a little as it tumbled to the valley floor far, far below.

"She's got her own fucking rocket launcher? Seriously?" Lethe said to anyone close enough to hear him. The only answer was a fresh burst of gunfire from the direction of the makeshift road. He flinched instinctively, but he wasn't the intended target. He tried to think. He needed to get Cathy and Beatriz to safety, but—

Where was Beatriz?

He looked around frantically for the woman.

She'd been right beside him a couple of seconds ago.

He couldn't see her.

A smooth-sided pebble of grief began to knot in his throat, sinking into his gut.

A muffled impact accompanied the sudden slump of a black-clad body hitting the ground five feet away from his hiding place. It was the same mercenary who'd stopped him earlier. He wasn't waving his gun anymore. He'd taken a hit in the right cheek which had opened a hole the size of a fist in the back of the dead man's skull.

Lethe scurried away a couple of feet, putting a little space between him and the corpse, trying to shelter Cathy at the same time. He peered under the bus. It was hard to see anything, but he thought he saw Morais's legs race by. A moment later, the Professor dropped down low. He saw the muzzle flare from a machine gun as she emptied her clip of bullets over the edge of the plateau. She reloaded with the same deft skill of his own teammates. This wasn't her first rodeo. The realisation made him more uncomfortable than ever. Who was this woman?

More of her hired guns returned fire. All in the same direction, converging on a single target. They'd moved out into the open, walking remorselessly forward as they closed in on their enemy.

Seconds later, it was all over, not with a scream but with a series of meaty thuds as the bullets found their mark. Their would-be assassin jerked and twisted, each impact making him dance like their bitch, until a final pirouette took him over the edge and out into the nothing.

Silence claimed the mountainside, all the more eerie for how quickly it owned the night.

Lethe sank to his knees. He wanted to lean forward and kiss the dirt; he wanted to stand up and scream his love of life at the heavens. When he finally gathered his wits long enough to look up, he saw Beatriz standing over him. He'd never been so happy to see anyone in his life.

"Señor Lethe?"

"I think you saved my life," he said.

She shook her head. "Oh no, not me. I didn't save anyone. You have Professor Morais to thank for that. I am just the cook," she replied with a self-deprecating smile.

"I think I love you anyway, Beatriz."

"That is very kind of you to say, Señor Lethe, but my heart belongs to another."

"Just my luck," Lethe said. He let her help him up. In turn, he reached out to help Cathy stand too.

"I'm glad to see you're still with us," Camilla Morais said, coming around the bus.

"Thanks to your rocket launcher. Where the hell did you get that?" Lethe asked.

Morais shrugged. "I was a girl scout. Always be prepared." she said. When Lethe didn't look satisfied, she added, "I knew the police have... had a helicopter."

"You expected another attack?"

She nodded. "That I did. These aren't the kind of people to just give up."

"What the fuck have you got me into, Prof?" Lethe rubbed at the thickening stubble along his jawline.

"Nothing Charles wasn't warned about," she said.

It wasn't the kind of answer he wanted to hear.

Beside him Cathy was visibly shaking. Shock. Beatriz tried to comfort her. What Lethe didn't like was the fact that Morais was completely unfazed by the night time raid. There was something off about the woman. Academics didn't live and die by the sword—or rocket launcher in this case. She turned her back on him and walked away, barking instructions to her men. She was comfortable giving orders. More, she understood the nature of combat in a way that betrayed military experience. She was interesting.

They had suffered losses. Three of the mercenaries were dead. The only blessing was that none of the survivors were injured, even Beatriz.

They were adding a lot of bones to the mountain. Best guess ten or more police-terrorists had gone down fighting.

Morais barked fresh orders at the mercs. Not for the first time, Lethe wished he had a better grasp of Spanish. She pointed to the corpses of friends and foe alike, no doubt ordering another 1000-feet freefall 'burial' for them in the waiting Urubamba River down in the valley below.

"I need to talk to you," Lethe said, walking up behind the Professor.

She didn't look around. "It will have to wait."

"No. It won't."

Morais sighed, but he wasn't about to be deterred.

"I want out," Lethe said.

Now he had her attention.

"What?"

"Out. I'm not staying here. I'm going to send word back to Nonesuch for extraction. This isn't me. Whatever's really happening here, I'm not prepared to die for it. You can find some other idiot."

"We need you," she said.

"I really couldn't give a shit, Prof," he said, channelling his inner Noah. "No lost city of gold is worth this."

"I can't pretend I am not disappointed, Mister Lethe. Surely you must have known there would be risks when you signed up for this?"

"That's just it," Lethe said, letting his rising anger punctuate his point. "I didn't sign up. I'm not a field agent. I don't leave the house. I'm support. You sent our only field agent away."

Morais's confused expression turned to disgust.

"No, Mr Lethe. You cannot leave. Quite simply it is not safe for you to go back to Aguas Calientes. You are staying here where my people can protect you."

"You can't guarantee my safety here!"

"There are no guarantees in life. This matter is no longer up for debate." Morais turned her back on him.

"Fuck you. Just... fuck you," he muttered, walking away.

He needed Noah.

He retrieved the case containing his laptop. The latch had been tampered with.

"Cathy," he called across to the Canadian, who sat with her back to the rock face, staring out across the valley. She looked shell-shocked and seemed to stare straight through him. Lethe closed the case and took it over to her. "How are you doing?" he asked, hunkering down beside her.

"I'm not hurt," she said.

"I didn't mean physically," he said gently.

"I know."

"Did you see anyone messing with my case?"

She shook her head. "No. Why?"

He opened the case and groaned. "My satellite modem's missing."

She stared at him for a moment, as if considering how to answer. "Are you sure you packed it away?"

"Sure," he said. He was trying not to panic, but without it he was effectively cut off from the rest of the world, with no way to reach Noah. If he couldn't contact Noah, well he didn't want to think about how his friend would react to multiple missed check-ins.

"Guilherme?" he called out, seeing the Brazilian walking towards him. He had an assault rifle slung over his shoulder.

"Yes, my friend?"

"I don't suppose you moved my satellite modem for some reason?"

"No, sorry."

Lethe paused. "Did you see anyone messing with the equipment?"

Guilherme offered him a bemused expression for a moment and then said, "I'm not sure I understand. My English... is not always so good."

"That's fine," Lethe said unconvincingly. He was trying not to freak out, but the one piece of kit he needed to stay in contact with Noah and Nonesuch was gone. It hadn't just walked off the plateau of its own accord. He slumped down beside Cathy, feeling utterly deflated. He couldn't leave, he didn't want to stay, he couldn't call for help. What *could* he do? Go on strike?

He sighed.

Then without even thinking about he was doing, put his arm around Cathy. Halfway into the gesture—meant to offer her comfort, or him comfort, he wasn't quite sure—he realised what he was doing and almost stopped, self-consciously.

She rested her head on his shoulder.

They sat together in the semi-darkness.

"Looks like you're stuck with me," Lethe said.

"I'm glad," she said, but he wasn't entirely convinced she meant it. Yet she had her head on his shoulder. Were Canadians well known for sending mixed messages?

Lethe tried to stay in the moment—he was on a mountainside in the middle of an incredible landscape with his arm around a beautiful woman who said she was happy he was there—but all he could see were the sightless eyes of the dead mercenary. Using his free hand, he took off his glasses. The tremor in his hand was so slight he wouldn't have noticed it without the frame exacerbating the effect.

TEN

Dawn arrived, rich and red across the mountaintops.

Lethe continued his work in silence.

He wasn't in the mood for conversation. None of them were. The bodies from last night's ambush were gone, consigned to the river. The splashes of blood in the dirt and on the rocks, and of course the red stains on his clothes, weren't the only reminders of what they'd been through, but he chose to ignore the bullet holes in the side of the bus and deep scars in the plateau's rim where the helicopter's wreckage had carved a gulley on its way down.

He ate Beatriz's breakfast as he worked.

There was almost no taste to it; though whether that was because of what he'd been through or because Beatriz had finally exhausted her ingredients, he couldn't tell.

He was desperate to be gone, and the frustration of being unable to leave just made things worse.

The only bright spark in this horrific experience was Cathy.

She sat by the edge of the plateau, feet hanging over the precipice as she stared out into the morning mist. A white haze gathered lazily around the mountain peaks. Cathy looked up as Beatriz approached with a plate of food. She smiled, taking it, and the plump Peruvian lady returned to the makeshift stove. Lethe focused on the fact that the sooner he found the entrance to the hidden chamber, the sooner he could leave. He threw himself into his work.

Now he knew what he was looking for, and configuring the equipment was second nature. He didn't need Guilherme's help any more, either. By spreading out the scanner array he was able to cover a much larger area.

He had already mapped five square feet of the rock face by mid-morning, which is when the small army arrived.

Lethe watched five four-by-fours climb up the mountainside. They parked up alongside the bus. The plateau was large, but with the bus, the jeep, the police car and now five more bulky four-by-fours, it was getting crowded.

Each vehicle held another five armed men. Ronan called mercenaries 'Lego soldiers'. It was a joke. He said they played at war, like kids, with no personal stake in the battle. Now that they had disembarked, Lethe realised the new arrivals were not just men. There were five women in the crew of twenty-five. They were dressed in regular clothes, but kitted out with a frightening array of hardware.

He didn't feel any safer for their presence.

"More toy soldiers?" Lethe said as Cathy wandered over towards his table

"Morais hired them."

"How? She never left the dig? And who picked them? It's like there's an endless supply of guns for hire here. How do we know they are who they say they are? Have they told us who they are? They might be Shining Path police? And how is she paying for all of this?"

Cathy didn't seem all that keen on answering his barrage of questions, but said, "She has a guy. He hires the protection details."

Lethe didn't buy it.

Morais greeted the new arrivals warmly, with hugs and a few backslaps.

It didn't take an expert in body language to work out she knew them all—all twenty-five of them—which meant one of two things: either they were regular hires whenever the Prof was in Peru, or they were some kind of private army that answered to Morais. Watching the way they interacted there was no doubting the fact they were absolutely loyal to her. She wasn't even being subtle about it any more.

One woman waved to Cathy, who half-held up a hand in response.

It was a small thing, but it confirmed Lethe's suspicions.

He watched as the newcomers greeted Beatriz and Guilherme as warmly as they had the Professor.

Three of the men unloaded fresh supplies, two more brought equipment from their cars. The rest spread out to cover points high and low, relieving the original mercenaries with high-fives and fist-bumps.

The old guard took the opportunity for a break.

Morais returned to Lethe and Cathy, her arms wide, as if to say: *see, I have kept my promise, I have protected you.*

She was smiling. Lethe didn't share her enthusiasm.

"We are safe," she said. "And we have more food, more equipment, more fuel for the generators, and the explosives have arrived. Find our entranceway, Mr Lethe. Then we can all go home."

Whistling a few bars from *Rich Girl*, Lethe turned his attention back to the image on the laptop.

He could see her glare reflected in the screen. The smile remained fixed on her lips. "Do we have a problem, Mr Lethe?"

"No problem," he replied.

"Good. I am not a fan of problems."

Morais left them to continue supervising the unloading operation.

He felt Cathy's fingers in his as she took his hand. He squeezed. She squeezed back. There was no comfort in it.

Lethe was sure of it now. They were prisoners.

ELEVEN

Noah had been in Lima for two hours and twenty-seven minutes.

He was his losing patience with the bullshit already.

Carlos started by bringing him to a small terraced house in a narrow alleyway off a main street that looked like it would have been at home in a Lowry painting, such was the air of poverty and gloom that clung to the place. The row of houses was daubed a pale, patchy blue on the ground floor and a variety of bright colours on the second. The paint itself was thin and had flaked away in several places where decay had undermined it. There were cobbles beneath his feet. A single gutter ran down the middle of the alleyway, the camber dipping towards centre. Beyond the last house in the terrace, an arch led to a narrower alleyway.

A statue of the Virgin Mary lurked in an alcove at the arch's highest point, a religious mugger threatening to beat the unsuspecting traveller over the head with her prayers.

Each front door was squashed up close to the next, and most of the windows in between were set with black-painted iron bars. Those, too, had seen better days. They were flaked with rust.

Noah had given Carlos simple instructions: take me to a connected man. Every place had them, someone the locals looked up to, either out of fear or respect. *Barrios Altos* was no exception. The man spilling out of the stuffing-shredded chair in front of them was huge. Not just overweight, there was enough fat under his skin to make three people. Emilio Huerta. King of the Barrios. The fat man wore a string vest and cargo shorts and dripped sweat in the humidity of the afternoon. His lips curled around the cigarette fused permanently to his bottom lip. His runt stood beside him. An enforcer who was ninety-five percent skin and bone, four percent muscle, with that extra one percent of crazy it needed to keep the locals in line. He watched Noah, not liking what he saw. There was a pistol tucked into his waistband. The runt made no attempt to conceal it.

Noah noticed that every time Carlos mentioned *los científicos desaparecidos*, Huerta shook his head. He waved a fat arm ushering Carlos away. It was obvious he was lying. It wasn't even offensive; it was just a game to the fat man. He didn't deny knowledge of the scientists. The subject didn't make him uncomfortable or cagey, he just had no interest in discussing it. There wasn't enough money to buy what he knew, Noah read that in his body language. No translation necessary.

After five minutes of this, Noah finally snapped.

He pulled his own gun, his trusty Heckler and Koch USP 9mm, and took four steps forward, not rushing, smiling as he reached Huerta's side and jammed the muzzle up against the folds of fat beneath his face. The skinny enforcer moved fast—faster than Noah had anticipated, but Noah was faster. He didn't even look. He lashed out with the heal of his left hand, straight-arming the guy in the throat. He went down like he'd been shot. "Up," Noah said, pressing the muzzle uncomfortably deep beneath the folds of skin.

Huerta did as he was told, struggling like a beached whale to lever himself up out of the chair.

He looked like he really wanted to hurt Noah.

That made Noah happier than it had any right to. He liked when people let their emotions rule their actions. It meant they'd lost before they even started.

He bullied the fat man through a beaded curtain into the tiny kitchen beyond.

It smelled like shit in there; some kind of offal on the gas burner.

He slammed the big man into the ancient oven.

Pots and pans crashed to the concrete floor as the fat man struggled to stay on his feet. Deeper into the house, two elderly women screamed and yelled for help.

"Tell them to shut up or I'll put bullets in their mouths to make sure they can't say another word, *comprende?*"

He swore at Noah in a continuous stream of Spanish, then yelled something that shut the old women up.

"There's a good boy. See, that wasn't so difficult." In complete contradiction to his words Noah pressed cold metal of the gun hard into Huerta's flabby jowls. The fat man was raging inside, a furnace of emotions.

"Señor, what are you doing?" Carlos said, from the doorway. He hadn't followed Noah into the room.

"What needs to be done. Three people are missing and this piece of shit knows something. He's going to tell us or I am going make him watch while everyone he loves suffers for his silence. Bastards like this only understand one language: violence. Now, tell him if he doesn't spill his guts I'll put a bullet in each of his kneecaps then go and rape his mother back there while he bleeds and begs for his life."

"I can't say that!"

"Tell him, Carlos. Exactly that."

Carlos did not have to translate.

Huerta understood the threat.

"*Iras al infierno y yo te mandaré ahí!*" he said, spitting a wad of tobacco-yellowed phlegm at Noah.

He missed.

Noah pressed the barrel of the gun against Huerta's sweaty forehead.

Carlos eyed the door nervously. It was painfully obvious he wanted to be anywhere but here. "Ask your question again," Noah told him.

Carlos repeated his question about the missing scientists in Spanish.

This time the fat man glared his contempt at Noah. But his answer was different. Noah caught two words that told him all he needed to know: *Sendero Luminoso*. They were surrounded by a string of sounds that meant absolutely nothing to Noah, but he didn't need to understand them to know the fat man was spilling his guts. The last thing he said was, "*La Quinta Heeren.*"

"You know where he's talking about?" Noah asked Carlos, guessing somewhere in the babble of words was a place.

"Si. Yes."

"Good. Tell him thank you for his co-operation, and that I'm glad things didn't have to get ugly. I have no desire to sleep with his mother, not that she isn't a very attractive woman, I'm sure," Noah said. The translation was considerably shorter than that. Noah wasn't about to leave a pissed off gangster at his back, that was how you got shot walking away. Instead, he flipped the gun around in his grip, and in one fluid motion pistol-whipped Huerta across side of the face, breaking his jaw.

The fat man hit the ground and was smart enough not to move. "Come on," he told Carlos. "Take me where I need to go. Let's get this thing done and get back to the mountains. I've never liked cities. They're shitholes."

Noah walked back to the main street, aware that eyes were on him, watching from behind curtains. Let them watch. Let them remember him. It would make it so much easier if he had to come back to this place because the fat man had been stupid enough to lie to him.

No one lied to Noah Larkin twice.

"I never see anything like that," Carlos said, coming out of the house behind him. "That was... harsh. I thought you were really going to do those things you said."

"Who said I wasn't?" Noah said drily.

"You know that we are *muertos caminando* now?"

"Of course we are, *hombre*," Noah said. He had no idea what the phrase meant.

"That is not a good thing."

"Of course it is. No one forgets the *muertos caminando*."

TWELVE

Lethe couldn't get a signal.

Varying his break-time wander didn't help. Walking away from the dig site made no difference. Without the satellite modem there was no signal. He switched off the phone to conserve its battery life. It didn't take a genius to know Morais had taken his satellite modem. She didn't want him talking to the outside world. Well, fuck her and the horse she rode in on. He needed to get back to the town. Even if he couldn't get coverage on his mobile, the hotel should have a landline.

Guards were posted everywhere – he couldn't think of them as hired guns now, they were warders. He could feel them watching him constantly. He should have been flattered they considered him of value – at least that meant they were unlikely to shoot him. That didn't mean he could stop cooperating, though. There were other ways to keep him in line. Lethe was under no illusions about his own pain threshold. He wasn't Konstantin Khavin, who had on more than one occasion endured hours of the most brutal torture, including waterboarding, without cracking. He wasn't Orla, who had been through hell and come back. He wasn't Frost who had grown up on the streets of Ireland during the

Troubles and played both sides. He would last about thirty seconds. If that.

So his safest bet was to cooperate.

For now.

Once they found the entrance and pried it open, people would have other things to worry about than watching over him. He was banking on the treasure to buy him his freedom. All he needed was a minute, maybe two, with people looking the wrong way. He didn't relish the idea of driving down that crumbling mountain track, but fleeing over the mountains on foot was out of the question.

The problem was, once he found the way in to their precious treasure chamber, his usefulness came to an end.

Somehow he needed to hit the sweet spot, drag it out just long enough for Noah to get back here—assuming he figured out Carlos was dirty and didn't end up dead in some Peruvian back alley—and the pair of them could do the whole Butch and Sundance thing, but hopefully with a happier ending.

Or maybe not.

Lethe went back to work. If he was going to make a move it needed to be tonight. The idea of driving down the mountain in the dark was terrifying, but it was his best shot at getting away.

Right up until the moment he found the entrance.

The readings were unmistakable.

It crossed his mind to hide them, but Morais wasn't an idiot. She was checking his progress, looking at his results, and asking questions. It would take her no time at all to see he was lying. So, in the interests of self-preservation, he called her over.

"I've found it," he said. His lack of enthusiasm confused Morais.

"Found what?"

He nodded. "Take a look for yourself."

He made room for Morais to sit at his computer. She double-checked his results, a smile spreading over her lips. Lethe eyed the handgun tucked into her belt. Because of the strap slung over her shoulder the rifle would be impossible to grab without it turning into a wrestling match, but the pistol? The thought was fleeting. There and gone. He imagined her as his hostage, buying him his safety down the mountain as his human shield. But before he could make a grab for it, Morais stood up again and the moment was gone.

That moment of hesitation, of imagining instead of doing, was the difference between him and the rest of the old man's people. Frost would have seized that chance in a heartbeat, no second thought. Orla wouldn't even have waited for the moment: she'd have created her own. But Lethe was Lethe, not Orla, not Frosty. And Lethe had just let his best chance of getting out of here slip through his fingers.

He was pissed at himself.

He couldn't even take comfort in the fact he was beginning to think like a field agent.

"Guilherme!" she called. "I need you to look at this."

The Brazilian dropped what he was doing and came over to her.

He stared at the monitor, nodding to himself, then grinned, clapped his hands and laughed, a real hearty laugh. "Good job, my friend," he told Lethe, slapping him on the back. He traded a brief exchange with Morais in Portuguese that Lethe had no way of following. She hurried over to the rock face. Guilherme used the image on the monitor to guide her, edging her slowly left and left until she was in position to draw a big chalk X on the rock.

A collective cheer rang out.

Excited word spread. They'd found the way in.

Guilherme turned his broad smile on Lethe and raised his hand for a high five. "Don't leave me hanging," he said. Lethe played along with a forced smile.

He didn't get it. The team still treated Lethe like one of their own, but the mercs handled him like a prisoner. He couldn't read Morais. She flipped back and forth on a dime, reflecting his own uncertainty rather outing herself as the enemy here. It was only when he mentioned returning to the hotel, or reaching out to Sir Charles or Noah that the veneer cracked. She didn't even bother with excuses any more, she just said no.

Was that enough to make her an enemy though?

Or was she just being ultra-cautious given how much was at stake here?

Only one way to find out, he heard the voice of Noah inside his mind.

His capacity for self-preservation trumped his fear. He walked over to Morais, and asked her outright: "So, now you're done with me, I guess you either shoot me or send me home? Which one is it, Prof?"

Morais looked up from the detonator she was wiring.

"I'm kind of busy right now, Jude," she said, not looking up from the task.

"Don't you think I have a right to know? I've done what was asked of me. Can't you just put me on a train back to Lima."

"I can't spare anyone to take you."

No apology. He didn't buy it. She had an army of people up here. Any one of them could have driven him down the mountain. Lethe pressed on. "At least give me your phone so I can check in with Noah, let him know we've found the way in."

"The battery's dead. And why on earth would I want to shoot you? You are far too much fun to have around." She offered him a smile and for a moment he thought she might actually mean it. "Go, get something to eat. Catch up on some sleep. You've done good work here, Jude. I appreciate it. You may just have saved those people's lives. Take a moment to feel good about that."

It took Morais and Guilherme an hour to set up the explosive chain and the detonators. Watching him work, Lethe realised this was Guilherme's true field of expertise. He'd never operated the GPR in his life, and if it was stolen from the original team, well that might explain why some parts were missing.

He joined Cathy. She seemed every bit as miserable as he was. He wondered about taking her with him when he made his move, then found himself thinking three steps beyond that and trying to work out from the things he remembered about her interactions with the others if she could be trusted. He really was thinking like an agent instead of a desk jockey.

"I want to go home," he said to her. It was easy. Honest. Everyone knew he wanted out, he'd made no secret of it.

"Me too."

"Really? I thought you'd be dying to see what's waiting in there?"

She shrugged. "I think you'll be disappointed."

"How so?"

"Wait and see."

Guilherme gave the signal; the charges were in place and rigged to blow. He backed away from the rock face.

Morais held up a hand, signalling the soldiers to clear the ridge above the plateau.

Lethe picked up his laptop and retreated to a point of safety beside the bus. Beatriz and one of the guards were already there. Cathy joined them.

Morais's hand came down sharply, and the sound of the detonation echoed back to them two-fold, the echo multiplied by the mountains around them. The explosion itself was a disappointment. Guilherme had done his job well, the blast zone was localised, and the C4 had made minimal impact on the surrounding rock.

In the centre though, a dust cloud was settling around shards of stone.

Lethe could make out the outline of an iron door.

He couldn't help himself; he smiled. He was on the money. Those scans hadn't shown densely packed Inca stonework, they'd revealed the metal case of a man-made tomb inside the mountain.

Nobody else seemed surprised by the sight of the door, or what it meant, which as far as he was concerned was a dead giveaway.

The door itself was just about big enough to accommodate an elephant.

Guilherme returned from one of the four-by-fours carrying a hand-held pneumatic drill. He lowered a pair of plastic goggles over his eyes and put on a pair of ear defenders. The cans were huge, and made him look like a Cyberman. He fired up the drill and set to work on the rock face, removing the remaining splinters of stone that obstructed the newly revealed door. The drill was louder than the earlier detonation was. With the drill bit biting deep the shrill shriek of the metal boring into the rock reverberated around the surrounding peaks. The noise must have carried *miles*.

Chunks of rock spun away from the door and fell at the Brazilian's feet. Morais put a hand on Guilherme's shoulder. He killed the drill. Silence took longer to return than Lethe would have expected.

"There," Morais pointed at a point on the metal. Lethe stepped forward to better hear what she had to say. Cathy was a couple of steps behind him and behind her, one of the mercs. There was a keyhole in the door, he saw. It wasn't large, but the shape and function was unmistakable.

"Don't suppose you've got a key?" Lethe said.

Her answer was a question to her man. "Can we blast it?"

"Not now," Guilherme replied. "All charges gone. We have to get more. Another blast might bring down the mountain on top of us, and is not going to dent the door."

"Bollocks," Morais grunted, sounding decidedly British in that moment. Lethe almost smiled. "Get the old man," she said then, and Lethe was sure he was saved. Sir Charles was in on this, whatever this was.

The soldier handed Morais the satellite phone, which was quite obviously fully charged and working just fine.

"Quiero hablar con el anciano," she said into the mic. She paused, waiting on someone at the other end, then began again. "Herr Dreschner? I trust my people are treating you well?" Without waiting for an answer, she continued, "We found your door, right where you promised, however you neglected to mention anything about needing a key? That was most remiss, but I am willing to believe that it was a simple oversight on your part and not a deliberate attempt at sabotage." There was no doubting the threat in that last sentence. So, Lethe, reasoned, whoever Dreschner was, the 'old man's' circumstances mirrored his: a consultant-come-prisoner. "No doubt you assumed you would be rescued before we breached the mountain, but sadly for you, the police are quite inept. Now, if you would be so good as to tell me where we might find the key? It really would be a terrible shame if something were to happen to that delightful granddaughter of yours."

It was obvious she didn't care if Lethe was listening.

She might not be Shining Path, but she *was* a kidnapper and an extortionist. There was only one person here who could possibly have passed for a delightful granddaughter. The tears in Cathy's eyes confirmed his guess. She was trying desperately to hear the old man's voice on the other end of the line, even though it was pointless even trying.

"Porra!" Morais barked into the handset. "You have quite the sense of humour, Herr Dreschner. In other circumstances I like to think we might have been friends. No, I know," she said in answer to something he said, probably telling her to go to Hell. "As it is, you are lucky that you are old, my friend. I'd have you dig the door out with your bare hands and watch you scratch and claw at it until your fingers bled. Your granddaughter though, well, she is not so lucky." She broke off to look at Cathy. "Yes, yes, she's still very much alive. She's even found a new friend. Would you like to talk to her? Good. Tell her where to find the key. It will keep her alive longer than anything else you might have to say."

Morais handed the phone to Cathy, who took it with a trembling hand. "Grandfather? Yes, yes, I'm fine. I promise you. No, she hasn't hurt me. She's been good to me. But please tell me where you have hidden the key. You have to believe me. She will kill me if you don't."

Lethe listened, all thought of escape banished from his mind.

"Thank you, grandfather. I love you. I want you to know that. More than anything. You are my world. Yes. I will tell them. Goodbye." She handed the phone back to Morais.

"I hope you told her everything," Morais picked up without missing a beat. "Good day, Herr Dreschner. It has been a privilege knowing you." It sounded like a death sentence to Lethe. Morais killed the satellite phone and turned her attention to Cathy. "Where is it?"

"They buried it at Machu Picchu. He didn't know exactly where. It was sixty years ago, and they had been on the run from the Peruvian government at the time. The site had been undergoing reconstruction. All he remembers is that the key was hidden within the walls of a storage house on the east slope. He can't be more specific than that."

For some reason Lethe had assumed the ruins of Machu Picchu were in their original state, untouched since they'd been discovered. What was this 'reconstruction' she had mentioned?

"Castillo," Morais turned to one of the grunts, "Tell the others we're returning to the hotel. Guilherme, start packing up the equipment. Jude, I need you to modify one of the scanners to detect small metal objects."

"Why not use one of the metal detectors?" Lethe asked.

"Too large an area to cover, and not enough time to investigate all of the false positives they'd turn up. The GPR has the benefit of identifying what we're seeing before we knock any walls down."

"I'm not sure," Lethe said, "The scanner's images aren't that clear."

"But they are better than nothing."

And having a job to do kept him useful, and being useful kept him alive until Noah could get back.

"What about me?" Cathy asked.

"I don't need you anymore, my dear," Morais replied, quite reasonably.

Cathy looked panic stricken. "What? But—"

"We know where the key is, and with that knowledge your use to us comes to an end."

"Professor, please! I can help you. Grandfather won't tell you anything if I'm dead."

"I doubt very much there is anything he could tell us now we can't work out for ourselves, and should we need to ask him, well, we'll just have to make sure he doesn't find out you are no longer with us, won't we?"

Morais took out her gun.

Lethe was caught in a moment's indecision. He wanted to put himself between the two of them, but he wanted to stay alive more.

It was a bluff. It had to be. Surely Morais wouldn't shoot Cathy in cold blood?

"I did what you asked. I kept my head down. I didn't cause trouble. I even kept Jude distracted like you asked me to. Please."

Lethe froze.

Everything here was a lie, even her head on his shoulder.

But that didn't mean she should die.

"Fuck it," he muttered, and put himself between them. "You don't need to do this. She can help me. Two pairs of eyes are better than one."

"Touching," Morais mocked. "But ultimately pointless. Stand aside, Mister Lethe."

"No."

"I said stand aside."

"And I said no. One syllable, not so difficult to understand. My mum told me it was the first word I learned. Not daddy, not mummy. No. It's always been my favourite word."

He willed himself not to flinch as Morais raised her hand; he expected the pistol-whip but it didn't come. She lowered the gun.

"You're a fool, but you are right, there is a way I can use her still. If you even so much as *think* about escaping, I shoot her. Understood? Her life is now in your hands. You defy me again, I let Castillo's men have their fun and then I shoot her. Okay?"

"Sounds almost reasonable," Lethe replied, trying to keep his voice steady.

"Good. Start packing up," said Morais. "We'll return to the hotel and you two can get to work on adapting that scanner."

Lethe let out a sigh of relief as Morais moved off.

Cathy put a hand on his arm. "You didn't have to do that," she said. "I don't know how to thank you."

"Forget about it." The hand tremors were worse this time. He didn't need the glasses to see them.

"I'm sorry. I am. I didn't want to help her. But I had to. But that doesn't mean I didn't enjoy talking to you. I just..." She was running out of words, and not really explaining herself, which was understandable all things considered.

"It's fine," Lethe lied. The truth was it hurt, but at least he knew he could trust her. Unless Morais threatening Cathy's life was just another layer to an elaborate charade?

THIRTEEN

"There's something that's been gnawing away at me for a while, hombre. I'm hoping you can put me straight?" Noah Larkin said. He handed the binoculars to Carlos. The Prof's man took his turn to scan the perimeter of La Quinta Heeren. It was a relatively opulent two-storey building out of keeping with many of the streets around it. The house occupied the corner of a large square plot of land. It was flanked on two sides of a smaller, well-kept square garden surrounded by waist-high iron fencing.

"I can't promise that," Carlos said. "Try me."

"Okay, my understanding has always been that the Shining Path kept to rural areas. They're not exactly known for attacks on urban areas. So riddle me this: why would they suddenly decide to hide three American hostages so close to the city centre?"

"Historically, they have, I'm not sure how you say it? Got more people?"

"Recruited?"

"Si, in the past they recruited their people from the country regions, where the poverty and unrest was more obvious, but they have always been in our cities. The killings of '91? You heard about these?" Noah nodded. "They happened just a few blocks from here." Carlos indicated beyond the houses to the right.

It wasn't an uncommon story when it came to anti-terrorism: Government ops had stormed the first floor of a building in Barrios Altos and massacred fifteen people, believing them to be the leaders of the Shining Path. The problem was their intel was fucked up. Their marks were on the second floor. The fifteen dead people were innocent victims of a colossal fuck up. The raid had gone down a few blocks from the parliament building.

Their current locale offered an unobstructed view of La Quinta Heeren; certainly as good a view of the square as was possible. He watched as a couple of tourists posed for pictures. There was a serenity to a place like this that belied its proximity to the Barrios. There was old wealth here.

Without Lethe in his ear to provide satellite-guided information, Noah felt blind. Normally he'd be getting a constant babble about the number of people inside, breakdowns of their heat signatures and their positions, movement, comms and just about anything else his eyes in the sky could sniff out. But there was something cathartic about doing this the old fashioned way. It was years since he'd been on a stake out. One thing his days as a sniper had given him was patience. He could wait forever for the right shot. Carlos, on the other hand, was bored out of his tiny mind and itching to do something.

"Sit tight. All we've got to do is wait. Nothing more than that. Just sit. Wait. And not fuck it up by getting impatient. Sooner or later one of them is going to leave, whether it's for a cigarette, to buy some milk or run some kind of errand. They don't know we're watching, so for them it's just business as usual. When they're exposed, we follow and grab one of them.

We get what we need to know out of them with a few simple questions and take it from there. What we don't do is go storming in all guns blazing. That's the short cut to winding up dead."

Carlos listened to Noah. He didn't disagree, but it was obvious sitting on his hands was driving him not so slowly crazy.

"Yes, yes, of course. You are wise," Carlos said, "But one problem: by the time your plan is done, Señor, the hostages will be dead. They're going to kill them soon, and put the video on the internet as a warning to others who do on heed their demands. And that is ignoring the fact that Huerta will not sit idly by. His people will be looking for us."

"All the more reason to keep our heads down," Noah said.

While Carlos and his friends displayed surprising competence for hired guns, it was obvious they the lacked patience of an old hand. Too many soldiers were in a hurry to get dead as far as he was concerned. But he grudgingly admitted Carlos had a point.

And it was stupid to ignore local intel during an active op. Carlos said the kidnappers were going to start putting execution videos online, ISIS style, and Noah was inclined to believe him. He wasn't worried about Huerta. He could handle anything that fat bastard had to throw at him.

"I say we walk up and knock on the front door. They open it up all smiles thinking we are pizza delivery and we start shooting. It doesn't have to be complicated."

As far as plans went, that certainly wasn't complicated, but it wasn't happening, either.

The problem was Noah was reckless. He always had been, and without Lethe in his ear telling him to wait it out, part of him quite liked the idea of helping things along. Not that he intended to rush in blindly and get himself and the hostages killed.

"Ah fuck it, let's have some fun, shall we?" Noah drew his Heckler and Koch USP 9mm. It felt right in his hand, like an extension of his fingers and palm, and he drew strength from it. It was the most reliable gun he had ever used, typical German attention to detail, and he owed his life to the weapon's uncanny ability to work perfectly every time, even under extreme conditions, with minimal maintenance. He may be about to do something stupid, but he knew he could handle it.

Carlos carried an AK-47, which as far as Noah was concerned was like bringing a sledgehammer into a china shop. Still, there was a reason why it was the most popular assault rifle in the world. Sometimes precision wasn't necessary, thunder was, and the AK brought the thunder. More important though in terms of how the next few minutes would play out was the fact that Noah knew he could trust Carlos to stay calm under fire. He'd more than proved himself up on the plateau.

Keeping their bodies and weapons low, the two men raced across the courtyard.

The tourists had moved away, leaving them alone.

It was reasonable to assume the terrorists had eyes on the square, but if they were positioned up on the tower a bit of basic Pythagoras offered plenty of blind spots to make the approach. The viewing angle from up there wasn't great.

They reached the door without being riddled with lead.

Noah raised a clenched fist, the signal for Carlos to pause.

He listened intently for any hint of activity from within.

It was absolutely silent.

Eerily so.

He reached out for the iron handle and eased the door open a crack, listening intently.

Nothing.

It was dark inside, not pitch black, but dark enough to hide a lot of problems. He pushed the door wider, letting in the light. A musty smell greeted him as he crossed the threshold.

He moved out of the light, his back to the wall, and gave his eyes a second to adjust. To his left was a narrow corridor, he could just make out the darker shadows that he assumed were a number of doors leading off it, and the shadow of a staircase at the far end. To the right were a stack of small cages, each one empty.

He didn't like it.

Something didn't feel right.

It was too quiet.

Something else gnawed away at him, something intangible.

"I don't like this," he said, but Carlos was already away, checking the first room on the left-side hallway. It was a kitchen, nothing unusual in itself; pans hung from an iron rack on one wall, a wooden table dominated the middle of the room, a dozen chairs around it. There was an old-fashioned stove, a fridge.

But still it didn't feel right.

"We need to get out of here," he whispered.

But Carlos was having none of it. "And miss all the fun?"

He wasn't whispering. He aimed his AK-47 at Noah's face, taking a bead on his nose. Two more armed men moved into the space behind him. Three against one he could handle, at a push, with more than a slice of luck, but he heard more footsteps approaching.

"Oh you fucker, you got me, Carlos. I actually thought you were one of the good guys."

"I am," he replied, reaching out to take Noah's gun from his hand. "Now, on your knees. Let's not make this any more unpleasant than it needs to be."

Noah knew the drill. He put his hands behind his head, laced his fingers and dropped down. Hands grabbed his arms and twisted them painfully behind his back. Handcuffs snapped around his wrists.

He felt the sting of a needle puncturing the skin at the nape of his neck.

"Now, shall we go and visit the hostages you are so interested in, Señor Larkin?"

"Well, if we must."

FOURTEEN

There was one variable on the whole messed up equation he clung onto: the old man had willingly sent him here. Surely that meant that Camilla Morais had to be on the side of the angels?

Lethe sat in silence on the bus as it bounced down the mountain. The early morning drizzle fogged the windows. Morais had confiscated his phone – not that he could use it – his laptop, again useless without the satellite hook-up, and everything else he'd been carrying that could possibly have been used to send a message. Ten minutes with a laptop and a connection to the internet, Lethe could cripple the finances of a third world country. Give him a bit longer and he could probably instigate a regime change. But disconnected he was helpless.

It was humiliating.

He hated it.

And he wasn't stupid. He'd seen them. He could identify them. They knew what he was capable of. There was no way they were letting him go. The minute he stopped being useful was the minute he stopped being alive. So right now it was about finding a way to shape his own destiny; cause damage without being obvious. Give them a reason to keep him around.

That meant doing as he was told, and doing his best to keep Cathy safe. Noah wouldn't let him die out here. That was the other variable he clung to for dear life. If ever there was a free radical in human form it was Noah Larkin. Highly reactive and almost certainly short lived.

He was going to get time alone with the GPR scanner. He wasn't sure exactly what he could do with that time, but maybe there was a way to weaponise it or somehow use it to slip a signal out? Or maybe something as simple as getting his hands on some good old fashioned tools. Something to fight with.

It didn't take long for the master plan to hit a roadblock.

They'd allowed him to shower, they'd brought food up to the room, and then they'd set him to work. He wasn't alone. Cathy was with him and so, unfortunately, was Guilherme. The Brazilian watched him like a hawk, and questioned every single thing he tried to do. Every slight tweak or change to the configuration, he wanted to know what it did and how it changed the function of the machine. In the end, the best he could do was increase the range and field width of the scanner, and push the signal out on a higher frequency than the system would usually support, which, theoretically would reveal the highest resolution the GRP was capable of. It wouldn't set him free. He needed to rewrite code on the laptop, but without an internet connection there was no way he could send a digital message in a bottle out into the world.

So he tried to think differently, the Brazilian was a resource. He knew stuff they didn't. He tried to get him talking, but Guilherme refused to be drawn into anything beyond the scope of the GRP.

When it was finally ready they tested it on the walls. It was easy to identify the pipes hidden behind the plaster, and other metal pieces beneath the roughly painted surface, including screws and plates holding the baseboards together. It worked. How well it would work through the huge iron door was anyone's guess, but theoretically he'd done all he could.

Guilherme left, taking the scanners, the tools and any leftover parts with him.

In the half-second the door was open, Lethe clocked the armed guard standing watch. It had been unreasonable to hope they could just walk out the front door. The key turning in the lock ended that fantasy.

He was alone with Cathy.

Lethe crossed over to the single window. He didn't need to look out to discount it; iron bars prevented anyone from breaking in, they also prevented anyone from breaking *out*. He opened the window three inches, which was all the bars would allow. It was enough to let some fresh air in.

Cathy sat on the bed. She'd been crying. Her face was red and her eyes redder, but she wasn't crying now. He didn't try and comfort her this time.

"I'm sorry," she said. "About all this."

"It's not your fault. It's mine. It's Noah's. But most of all it's the old man's. He never should have sent me here."

"Well I'm glad he did. And no, I'm not flirting with you, or trying to be nice because she wants me to. I'm just glad I'm not alone."

"Let's change the subject. Tell me how you met the Prof?"

"She spent a year in Toronto. She was one of my lecturers at York."

"So she really is an archaeologist then?"

"One of the best. She's brilliant. Absolutely fascinating to listen to. But now I wish I'd left it there after the year was up. Stupid me, I jumped at the chance to come with her on a dig. I didn't think for a second she was Shining Path. She's not even Peruvian." She shook her head, annoyed with her own stupidity.

"What gave her away?"

"After she got thrown out of Peru the first time, I met up with her in Rio. She said she was coming back in, but using some of her underground contacts. They put us crates they usually fill with endangered animals to get us over the border. These weren't good people. They aren't. You've seen some of them for yourself. We met up with a small army in the foothills of the Andes. It was a wakeup call. I realised why Morais had been asking so many questions about my grandfather. And I knew why she had asked me to come on this dig. Looking back, I wouldn't be surprised if Morais did that entire year teaching just to get close to me."

"Who *is* your grandfather?"

"I don't know anymore. He's not Karl Dreschner whoever that is. It seems I've never known his real name. But he's always been the sweetest old man. I had no idea he was a... a Nazi war criminal. How could I know that?"

"A what?"

"After the war, a bunch of Nazis escaped trial and fled to South America. Grandfather was in Peru for a while before he settled in Brazil. He never speaks about his life before us. She's going to kill him, isn't she? He's ninety-five years old. He can barely see these days, doesn't have the strength to walk up and down the stairs at home."

"He's already dead. He was dead the moment she hung up the phone. Once someone outlives their usefulness they become a problem to be solved, and the easiest way to solve a problem is to end it."

"How do you know so much about her?"

Lethe shrugged. "I don't. Not her specifically. But this is what I do. This is the world I live in every day. People like her are obsessives. They're driven, single-minded, and ruthless to the point of being lethal. They leave a trail of corpses in their wake. It's how they stay hidden in plain sight. No one is left behind to talk about who they really are or what they've done."

"Have you lived through this kind of situation before?"

"Every time," he said, hoping it gave her a little hope. Hope was good most times. Unless it wasn't. Sometimes hope was an utter bastard. But as long as Noah was out there, unaccounted for, then hope was good as far as he was concerned. "This is nothing," he lied easily. "I've been in worse situations. Thing is we need to be smart. We can't just sit around and wait to be rescued. I'll get us out of here. Trust me, I'm good at this."

She nodded. He had no idea if he'd convinced her. He hadn't convinced himself.

She went into the bathroom, closing the door behind her.

"What the hell are you banging on about, you moron?" Lethe whispered at the face looking back at him in the silvered mirror. "'I'll get us out of here'? Trust me? I'm good at this? Christ I wish I had a computer."

"Did you say something?" Cathy called through.

"Just talking to myself. Nothing important."

FIFTEEN

Another day, another prison cell.

This one was underground, featureless, windowless and airless.

Not *literally* airless or he wouldn't be able to breathe, but he couldn't feel a hint of a breeze. Noah knelt beside one wall. His arms were pulled behind him, chained together. The chain was attached to a yoke on the wall, drawing his wrists painfully upwards. He couldn't move properly, and the weird posture was screwing with his circulation. There was no way to relieve the stress on his shoulders as his weight pulled his arms down. His range of motion was so limited he couldn't shift the crippling cramps setting in.

The only light came from a large gap beneath the door where the movement of shadows and the brief scurried sounds and snippets of conversation told him two men were on the other side.

It was pointless trying to keep track of time, almost as difficult, in truth as trying to come up with an escape plan.

But he hated being caged up and had no intention of staying that way even a second longer than he had to.

Still, small mercy, there were no rats.

He assumed he was still inside La Quinta Heeren, but it was possible they'd moved him to a secure location when he was out cold.

He shifted position again, trying to work some sort of feeling to his left leg.

The sensory deprivation of his confinement amplified the numbness whenever he shifted position. It should have been unbearable, but discomfort was good. Discomfort would keep him focussed. Focus would keep him alive. So he concentrated on every single inch of pain, welcoming it.

They wouldn't leave him alone in here forever.

Someone would come to feed him eventually.

They didn't.

He heard Carlos though the door, ordering the guards about in Spanish. A flurry of activity followed: he saw the shadows move under the door, heard footsteps and the scrape of a chair dragging back on the stone floor. A door opened somewhere deep inside the complex. A distant rattling of chains, like Jacob Marley trying to spook Scrooge into some Christmas spirit, and another voice, begging. He recognised the language. German.

"Food," Carlos said. "Don't be stubborn, eat it this time."

It was hard to make out the words, the speaker's voice was so frail. Either old or weak, or both. Noah caught what he thought was Cathy's name, but the door closed again before he could work out what was being said.

And still they didn't come for him.

He worked the muscles in his shoulders and back, then his hands, one finger at a time, concentrating on each as he curled and uncurled them.

They turned up later. A lot later. He assumed it was around three or four in the morning; that was how these people worked. Wait for a time when you were naturally vulnerable, come in with pain and the promise of release, then double down on the pain. There was no food for him. Instead they unchained him, hauled him up to his feet and dragged him out into the next room. He didn't waste energy fighting them. He focussed on the release of pain. The rush of blood was intense; a drug.

The new room was brighter, but still obviously underground.

He kept his head down, feigning weakness. Let them underestimate him at their peril.

Two men had Noah's arms. They spoke rapid-fire Spanish, back and forth, making no attempt to hide their faces. That was a bad sign. Chances of survival dropped exponentially when the kidnappers made no move to hide who they were—psychologically it meant they weren't expecting it to come back and bite them in the arse. Dead men tell no tales and all that crap. He noted a third man, armed with a submachine gun, guarding the staircase at the far side of the basement room.

The guards shoved Noah into a chair in the middle of the room. A television had been set up on a rough wooden table. The power cable snaked back across the bare stone floor to a single power point on the far side. One of the men shackled chains around Noah's wrists, binding them behind the chair. They didn't shackle his ankles. The two men stepped back. He could sense the tension in their bodies. Good. Let them worry about him.

Noah waited.

He gave them nothing.

He marked two closed doors. Behind one, the old German. He knew that much. Behind the other, the three missing scientists?

Before he could set himself to properly thinking about it and looking for any telltale giveaways, Carlos came down the stairs. He was carrying a laptop. He set it down on the table and opened it in front of Noah. Before he powered it up, he put a piece of paper in front of him. It was written in English. There wasn't a single word on it that surprised him.

"Now, my friend," Carlos said, the smile giving away the fact he was anything but, "In a moment we are going to put a call through to your boss."

"Are we now?"

Carlos nodded. "We are. And you're going to read the script I've written for you word for word. If you deviate in any way, Lethe dies. I'm not stupid enough to think threatening you will work as a motivator, but you seem to have a fondness for the nerd—"

"He's not a nerd, he's a geek, there's a difference."

"If you say so. I'm sure he will bleed just the same. So, read the script. Don't try and be cute."

Noah shrugged. "And what if he asks me questions?"

"You tell him you have to go."

"You think he's going to buy that?"

"It's up to you to sell it."

"Video?"

"Do you think I am stupid? No. Sound only."

The script left no room to improvise. But that didn't mean he couldn't work with it. The old man wasn't an idiot. He had to know he'd sent them into the lion's den here.

"Okay, do it."

Carlos placed the call.

The old man answered. "Who is this?"

Noah needed it to sound natural, but he just didn't talk like this. "Hey boss. It's me. I'm using Carlos's laptop to call you. I don't have long so just listen. I heard from Jude, he's fine. He says he's close to finding the chamber entrance. I've got a line on the missing Americans in Lima. I'm going to try to attempt extraction tomorrow."

"Should I make arrangements for backup?"

"It's all good, boss. Okay, got to go. I'll check in later."

Carlos clicked the button and the line went dead.

"Good, Señor Larkin. You sounded almost convincing. But those weren't quite my words, were they?"

"No. Your words were dumb. He knows me. He knows how I talk. I fixed them for you."

"I told you not to."

He was banking on the fact the old man would react to the brevity of the conversation. The question was, would it be enough to trigger a response?

And the answer was probably not.

Carlos closed the laptop.

"Hungry?" the Brazilian asked.

"No."

"You take all the fun out of life, Señor. Do you know that? I had been so looking forward to telling you there was no food for you today, or tomorrow for that matter, and there you have to go and ruin it." Carlos thought this was hilarious.

Noah said nothing.

"Take him back to the cell. We're done here."

SIXTEEN

This road wasn't any better than the last one.

The dizzying drop off the sheer cliff was vertigo-inducing, and the fact that the elevated bus seats masked the real distance between them and the edge enough that he effectively looked out over *nothing* didn't help. And this time there was traffic coming the other way. Like all the drivers in this godforsaken country they had a death wish, Lethe was sure of it. They tore along the dotted line in the centre of the winding descent as though they were trying to open a carton of milk. More than once Guilherme was forced onto the embankment, tires churning mud, to allow empty buses to pass by on their way to pick up more Machu Picchu bound tourists.

Even more ridiculous was the fact the walkers bisected every switchback of the climb. Their tired feet had carved out a channel in a straight line from the peak to the foot mountain. There was an inevitability about it, objects moving at different speeds, their trajectories intersecting. Eventually something was going to have to give. Rock beats scissors, it's also pretty good against busses and flesh come to think of it, Lethe thought, looking out of the window. He hated being alone with his thoughts. His fingers twitched, almost like they were playing an invisible piano. In truth he was tapping out keys in his mind, executing subroutines, not sonatas.

The early morning fog clung to the rolling mountain tops. As ever, the near-permanent drizzle misted the air. It condensed on the bus's windows. Behind them they'd got quite a convoy. They were followed by the jeep and two of the four by fours from the plateau. How they got to this place, considering there were no roads between Aguas Calientes and here was a different matter. It meant resources.

"There," Morais said, indicating a passing place on the side of the winding road. Guilherme steered the bus to a halt. The rest of the convoy pulled in behind him.

She turned to address the passengers: Lethe, Cathy, Beatriz, Guilherme, Castillo and half a dozen armed men and women. She spoke in Spanish. Lethe didn't need a translator this time. He knew what was going to happen. The bus would stay here to block the road while the rest of them headed up to the ruins.

They transferred to the cars.

Two of her foot soldiers stayed behind.

The three cars started up, pulling level with the bus. Words were exchanged through the window, then they moved on up the mountain as Guilherme botched a three-point-turn, angling the bus so that it completely blocked the road. He clambered out and jogged up the road to join them.

The two foot soldiers opened up the hood to get at the bus's engine block, creating the illusion of a perfectly reasonable breakdown. After all the bus was something out of the original Incan era, no one would be surprised to see the engine fuming.

Lethe lost sight of the bus as the car negotiated yet another switchback. He was sandwiched in between Cathy and

Morais, the GPR on his lap. Beatriz and Guilherme rode up front. He wasn't about to let the scanner out of his sight. If he'd screwed up his calculations, they were dead. That was stressful enough without worrying that someone might actually want him to screw up.

They continued up the mountain.

Lethe was really beginning to hate mountains.

The cars passed a hotel and a handful of small offices before drawing up at the visitor checkpoint. Morais's group had not booked tickets, but that wasn't going to stop them. Two police officers guarded the site while a third man checked the tickets. There was already a long line of visitors queuing to get in while others milled about, checking maps and taking pictures.

Castillo and three soldiers jumped down from the jeep. No one looked their way. They were just tourists. There was more to look at in every other direction, as the landscape captivated them. It also meant no one saw their death coming. Castillo opened fire. His bullets cut into the line. The soldiers beside him joined in the slaughter.

The two officers went down first.

Bullets tore into the first three tourists in the line, ripping through the thin fabric of their windcheaters. They went down. They had no time to realise they were dead before two more, a boy and girl no more than six or seven, joined them. Lethe felt sick. He yelled a warning no one needed. The mountainside was alive with screams as people panicked. None of them knew what to do. It was chaos. There was no cover, nowhere to hide. Some tried to put bodies between them and the slaughter, others stood rooted to the spot by the abject terror. None of them could comprehend what was happening. And those few seconds of disbelief were damning.

Castillo took aim, putting a dozen shots into the spine of a young backpacker, making his corpse dance before it fell.

The slaughter was ruthlessly efficient, and the site so remote no one was going to miraculously appear to save them. There was no point in even trying to hide. Castillo walked towards them, bringing death with him. Two young women fell to their knees before the mercenary, their hands up above their heads as they begged for their lives. They were pretty young things right up until the moment the bullets stole their faces.

Lethe didn't want to get out of the four by four. He didn't want to be here. He didn't know what to do. "Out," Morais ordered, again. He hadn't heard her the first time.

He shook his head.

"One last time, Mister Lethe, out, or I put a bullet between your eyes."

What would Noah do? The thought flashed across his mind. The answer that came with it was a simple one: get out of the car. He might not be able to save these people, but he could keep Cathy alive. That had to count for something. A small victory.

Noah would also make a mental tally of debts to be repaid, and every one of those bastards would pay for what they were doing sooner rather than later, when they were alone and vulnerable and least expecting it. Noah would come to them like a black angel and end them.

So that was what he was going to do.

Morais used a megaphone to drown out the cries of the dying and the sobs of those as yet unharmed. It was a short announcement delivered first in Spanish then repeated in English. "Ladies and Gentlemen, we are the Shining Path. Please get down on the ground and remain still. Failure to do so will result in your death. I have no wish to see more of you meet your maker, but I am pragmatic. This will serve as your only warning. There is nothing to be gained by dying a hero. I'm sure I don't need to say this, but I will say it anyway. No telephones or other mobile devices. Any attempt to record our activities here will result in the death of every single one of you. No exceptions."

She threw the megaphone into the jeep and barked out more orders.

Three of her men took up positions around the checkpoint.

Lethe stared at the Professor in horror. How could the old man fall for her? It didn't make sense. What did she have on him?

It occurred to him then that maybe, just maybe, the old man hadn't been blindsided. Maybe he'd known all along what kind of monster Camilla Morais was, and he'd sent them in here to put an end to her and the threat she posed. And that thought chilled him almost as much as the slaughter. Why no warning though?

Morais and Castillo led their remaining force through on foot. They didn't so much as acknowledge the cowering and sobbing tourists. They were irrelevant. Lethe caught the eyes of a few of them as he passed by. He saw fear and hate looking back at him and realised they thought he was the enemy. He wished he could tell them otherwise, but he couldn't risk giving them false hope.

His resolve shattered as he passed a man and two small children sobbing over the body of a woman. His wife. Their mother. Blood soaked her body from six wounds across her chest and neck. There was nothing anyone could do for her. *Keep fighting*, he told himself. *Fight for them.* His teeth gritted, he kept on moving, ignoring the devastated faces and desperate sobs.

Stay alive.

Beyond the gate, a narrow path split into two.

One route led upwards via stone steps. The group took the other path, marching on. Lethe knew the basic layout of the site from the map. The storage houses were the closest part of the ruin to the checkpoint. Despite the early hour there were a surprising number of people already exploring the site. They'd heard the gunfire, seen the armed men, but at least a few were smart enough not to run for the entrance, taking their chances with hiding out in the ruins. The rest would be mopped up by the men Morais had left behind at the checkpoint.

The vista might have been incredible, a genuine wonder of the world, but Lethe didn't care. He didn't care about the ruined city or the breath-taking mountains.

The site cascaded down the side of the mountain in terraces, giant steps that had once been the agricultural backbone of the city, like a giant's staircase descending to the valley below.

In the distance, he could see the city proper. The grey stone walls were like a maze viewed from above, but even from this shallow angle there was no denying the fact that they were impressive.

The storehouses were complete. They even had thatched roofs, which was a dead giveaway that they had been extensively reconstructed. Five of them stood in line. The slope was so steep that the roof of one storage house stood level with the base of the next.

"Start at the top and work your way down, Mr Lethe. I expect to hear the second you come across anything even vaguely interesting, understood?"

He nodded.

Morais had one metal detector, Guilherme another and they were obviously going to search down here while he worked up above them.

Three of the Shining Path soldiers shouldered their rifles and took compact sledgehammers from their backpacks. He saw that Beatriz carried one as well.

One of the foot soldiers escorted Lethe and Cathy as they ascended the narrow stone steps to the storehouse on the highest plateau of the agricultural zone. Beatriz followed them up.

Lethe moved the barrier designed to prevent public access and they went inside.

Gunfire erupted further down the slope.

It didn't last long. Three sustained bursts, maybe ten seconds. And that was the end of the police detail. He didn't need to be a genius to know who won; no one came to arrest them.

He set Morais's laptop on a stone bench and began the calibration process while Cathy and Beatriz positioned the scanner in the centre of the room. It took less than five minutes. To his stress-fractured mind it felt like five years.

It took three more minutes to scan the entire room: In that time the machine identified five possible metal objects hidden within the walls.

Cathy marked each spot with chalk.

Beatriz called Guilherme.

The Brazilian used his metal detector to confirm that Lethe had indeed found metal objects at three of the five places.

Beatriz took her sledgehammer and slammed it into the wall in the middle of the first chalk cross. A shower of dust descended from the ceiling as the impact shivered through the wall, but the structure held firm. She delivered three more crushing blows, and each one caused the wall to tremble. Still the interlocking stones refused to give.

"Here, let me try," Guilherme told her. Beatriz surrendered the sledgehammer to the Brazilian. He took five swings at the wall, each one doing damage to the straw roofing, but not so much to the stones.

Beatriz called for more soldiers.

Morais arrived with two of her men.

"We're not getting in this way, these walls aren't giving an inch," Guilherme complained. The head of Beatriz's sledgehammer rested on the earthen floor. He was breathing heavily already.

"You try," Morais said, stepping back so the first of her soldiers had room to swing.

First hit, nothing.

Second, nothing.

Third, nothing.

The man looked at Morais. She nodded, indicating that he should continue.

Fourth hit, the wall collapsed.

When it settled, Guilherme ran the head of the metal detector over the debris.

When he got a hit, he took a chisel from his belt and chipped away at a partially broken stone. A moment later his efforts revealed a small piece of metal. Lethe couldn't see it clearly, but it was almost certainly some kind of Incan jewellery.

It wasn't a key.

"Next one," Morais said.

Beatriz said something in Spanish to Morais. She agreed. Beatriz grabbed Lethe's arm by the elbow and pulled him back over to the GPR. His babysitter followed with Cathy in tow.

"Time to set up in house number two," she said to him. "No rest for the wicked. Let's go." Cathy picked up the scanner while Lethe took the laptop. The Shining Path men went to work on another chalk cross as they left.

The next building was similar in size, but had no roof.

Once inside they repeated the routine, turning up potential finds. Cathy marked them, and they moved on to the next storehouse. All the while, Lethe's armed babysitter kept a watchful eye on them. By the time they reached the lowest building, Morais and her team were still working at tearing down the walls in the second from the top.

Down here, at the lowest point of the giant's staircase, the four of them were pretty much on their own.

One of the Shining Path goons stood nearby on the steps, staring back towards the city for any signs of further resistance.

The only people paying any attention to Lethe were Beatriz and his babysitter.

He almost didn't do anything. He almost went ahead and let Cathy chalk up the last x's, but he knew when that happened his usefulness was over. This was it. Now or never.

"What the *hell* is that?" He barked, putting all of his pent up fear behind that one line. He thrust out a finger, pointing at some nebulous thing behind the guard. The man bought it, turning his head and half-stepping sideways, just enough for Lethe to rush him. He made a grab for the pistol stuffed into the man's belt.

He put it in the man's face, willing his hand not to shake.

"Don't even think about it," Lethe rasped. "Drop the rifle."

The soldier didn't flinch. He *chuckled* as he unslung the rifle from his shoulder.

Instead of dropping it, he swung the butt around, the impact knocking the gun from Lethe's grasp.

"Fuck," Lethe grabbed for it, but the chance was gone. The soldier had him by the throat.

Cathy picked up the fallen pistol and aimed it squarely at the guard. "Let him go."

"I don't think so." The man's accent was thick but his amusement was obvious.

Cathy tried to shoot him, squeezing down on the trigger while the muzzle veered frantically left and right. She couldn't get the gun to work.

"Oh, for fuck's sake," Beatriz said in perfect English.

She pulled a pistol and aimed it at the guard. This time he paid attention. "Hey, *compadre*."

Beatriz timed the shot with the hammer blows coming from the building up the hill, one shot opening up a third eye in the thug's head. The gunshot echoed loudly in the room, but the man went down without a sound.

Lethe stared at the cook, not understanding what had just happened.

"You must be the single most inept field agent I've ever had the misfortune to work with," she shook her head. "Come on, we don't have much time. This needs to be done right. A lot of lives are at stake."

Making sure nobody was watching them, they dragged the guard's body further into shadows inside the storehouse.

Beatriz claimed his submachine gun and handed Lethe her pistol. She led them back into the sunlight. Around the back of the storehouse a stone wall ran all the way up the terraces, forming a narrow staircase with stones arranged in crude steps.

"To be fair," Lethe whispered as he followed the dumpy Peruvian along the wall, "I'm not actually a field agent."

"Shut up unless you want to get us killed?" She whispered with so much vehemence Lethe couldn't do anything other than fall silent. "From here, you do what I tell you. No questions."

Lethe nodded.

He followed her, concentrating on not falling as they climbed the precarious steps.

Cathy brought up the rear, still carrying the gun she'd been unable to fire.

They paused behind the third storehouse. From their vantage point they couldn't be seen by the guard on the steps, but could see back as far as the visitor checkpoint. Beatriz ducked back as Morais emerged from the ruins of the second storehouse. Their voices carried, even if the substance of their words didn't. They entered the third storehouse, the thickness of the wall all that separated him from the terrorists. Hammer blows pounded against the stones just a few feet from his head.

"This way," Beatriz said.

They followed her along the path, away from the ruins. She moved fast for a woman of her size and age. Lethe struggled to match her pace.

A single guard stood on the path, his back to the ruins.

Beatriz waved Cathy and Lethe back into hiding.

The guard saw her.

Beatriz smiled back.

Oblivious to the very real threat she posed, the man stepped aside to let her through, and with blistering speed the older woman pivoted and cracked the butt of her gun across the back of his head.

The man dropped like a stone.

Lethe broke cover, guiding Cathy along the dirt path back to the checkpoint.

They moved fast and low, keeping a waist-level wall between them and the eyes at the entrance to the site. He saw Castillo moving through the frightened tourists. He didn't need to do a headcount to know there were at least a hundred of them. They were face down on the ground.

The sacred mountain was eerily quiet, aside from the regular hammer blows from the storage houses.

"When I give you the word, you've got one job, get her to a car," Beatriz said.

Ahead of them, Castillo answered his radio after a burst of static.

Beatriz translated: Morais had found the key and was telling her man to make preparations to move out.

Castillo signalled to his men, sending them back to get the cars running. They turned, presenting their backs. Beatriz seized the moment. She rose up from behind the wall and fired off two rounds. She was fifty yards from her mark. She didn't miss. Both bullets slammed into his spine.

The gunfire triggered more panic amongst the tourists. Tears. Sobbing. Mercifully, nobody stood up. Beatriz made her move. She ran forward, firing as she went, one measured shot after another. A black clad Shining Path fighter turned as she reached an SUV, taking a bullet to the face even as her comrade threw himself to the ground. He took cover behind the car, rising a couple of seconds later to return fire.

Beatriz kept coming, firing shot after shot as he popped his head up again. One of her bullets took the roof of his skull off.

She moved behind the checkpoint building, signalling to Lethe and Cathy to follow her. They kept the checkpoint between them and Castillo as Beatriz yelled out to the tourists. "Everybody stay down. It's important you remain calm. I'm with the police. We're going to get you out of here, but you've got to work with us. That means don't move." She repeated the message in Spanish and was busy translating it into French as more machine gun fire erupted from the SUV. The bullets sailed over her head harmlessly, but the shock of the gunfire had the hostages screaming again, undermining everything she'd said.

One young man tried to stand, only for a stray bullet to take him down.

For a moment Lethe thought they were going to get lucky, but this wasn't the day to buy any lottery tickets. Silence. Shock. And then mass panic rushed in to fill the void. First one then another and another surged up to their feet, running blindly. Another burst of gunfire erupted from the SUV.

"Idiots," Beatriz cursed. She yelled, "Get down!" But they weren't listening. The panic was contagious. More of them rose and started to run, even though there was no hope of them running far enough or fast enough to escape. There was no way off the mountain. She ran into the open, shoving her way through the terrified tourists as another man went down. This one clutched a hole in his throat as though he thought he could somehow stem the blood loss. Beatriz kept on pushing through. She couldn't stop now. Lethe and Cathy followed. It was pointless but she kept yelling at people to get down.

The Shining Path man had clambered up onto the roof of one of the four by fours and was firing indiscriminately into the crowd. Every bullet was intended to cause maximum damage. There was no way Morais hadn't heard the noise. The echoing gunfire matched the old gods throwing thunder between the mountains.

Beatriz didn't have a shot at the man on the roof, and wasn't going to get one without putting herself in the line of fire. Cathy did.

This time her gun fired.

The bullet took the soldier in the shoulder, spinning him sideways and backwards, but he didn't fall. The Canadian fired again. This time she missed. The bullet blew out the windscreen of the SUV. He returned fire. Bullets sprayed the wall beside Cathy's head. Lethe didn't think about what he was doing, he threw himself at her, dragging her down as the bullets cut through the wall where her throat had been. And then the firing stopped.

Beatriz finished him. One shot to the head. No mistake.

Cathy looked at Lethe lying on top of her. Before she could say anything Lethe said, "I don't usually get this close until at least the third date." Despite herself, she laughed. "We need to get these people out of here."

"No time," Beatriz snapped, hauling him to his feet. "Get to the jeep. Now."

They ran across the killing ground. Exposed. No shots rang out. Beatriz jumped behind the wheel and started the engine as Cathy clambered in beside her. Lethe threw himself into the back as the older woman floored the accelerator. The jeep shot away in a cloud of dust.

This time there was gunfire as Morais reached the checkpoint. Beatriz drove fast, taking each hairpin like a formula one driver. A backwards glance showed two SUVs churning up half of the mountain as Morais's people gave chase.

"We've got company," he yelled.

She didn't react.

The switchbacks sliced through the descent in a crazily steep zig zag, each bend turning back on itself in one-hundred-and-eighty-degree hairpins. One wrong turn, one slight misjudgement and they were off the road, and off the side. If they came off the tarmac, there would be nothing to stop them tumbling all the way down the mountain.

Lethe clutched the roll bar above his head as tightly as he could.

The jeep slid around another impossible corner.

He'd forgotten about the bus: it blocked the road almost completely. Beatriz had no choice but to slow down.

The two men they'd left behind to pretend to fix the bus made a show of looking under the bonnet. Three other people Lethe didn't know tried to help them. Beyond the stranded vehicle, Lethe saw three tourist buses lined up.

"Shit," Lethe said, the most eloquent word in his vocabulary at that moment.

They were pinned between their pursuers and the roadblock, no way forward, no way back.

They had seconds until the SUVs came thundering around the last of the hairpin bends.

The men at the front of the bus all looked up as they heard the engine approaching.

One of the Shining Path soldiers stepped forward, waving his arms to flag them down.

The other talked on his radio.

They knew.

In that second the man used his free hand to pull a handgun and aim it at the approaching jeep.

He opened fire as Beatriz shunted gears downwards. The jeep's transmission screeched as the first bullet skittered away off the nearside door. The vehicle lurched forward as she put her foot down. The second bullet struck the windscreen. The third shattered it.

Cathy screamed.

Lethe gripped the frame. He couldn't close his eyes. He couldn't tear his gaze away.

Beatriz barrelled towards the two men as they emptied their weapons onto the Jeep.

She didn't wait for them to get out of the way, and instead drove straight at them. One man went up over the bonnet and came down in a broken heap. Lethe wasn't watching him. He couldn't take his eyes off the bus still blocking their path.

There was no way around it, and no airbags to cushion the impact.

Wrenching the wheel to the right, Beatriz drove the jeep straight over the edge of the cliff.

SEVENTEEN

Time dilated as the jeep left the road.

He was dead. Trapped in limbo. Weightless.

But he couldn't let go, even as he was lifted out his seat. There was no road. No. There was something, a dusty path snaking down the steep decline. Lethe stared over Beatriz's head, down at the river in the valley far below.

A trail.

The wheels came down hard, hammering down on the track and bouncing back. The trail cut a swatch through the greenery, the straightest route down the mountain. Lethe's spine crunched as they landed from another jarring impact. The back wheels connected first this time, the jeep lurching into a dizzying angle as it ploughed through greenery, and still they hurtled downwards.

The jeep skidded, tipping up onto two wheels as Beatriz wrestled with the wheel, struggling desperately to find a way back onto the walking trail.

This time he did close his eyes.

The trail transformed into hundreds of stone steps.

Lethe felt every single one of them.

Up ahead two hikers scrambled to get out of the way. Trees crowded in around them now; they ploughed into the forested region too fast to stop. Beatriz didn't miss a beat, she used the gears to slow the headlong chase, but it barely made a difference as they burst from the trees and skidded across the next loop of the main road, then they were back into the trees again, and again in a breathless zig zag and then they plunged back under the canopy of foliage.

The trail, such as it was, was much narrower and the state of it deteriorated the closer it came to the bottom. It cut into a gully with high banks on either side of them. It was a tight fit. Beatriz scraping the jeep up against the side twice; any narrower and they were going to be stuck like a cork in a bottle.

The jeep grazed up against the wall again. Beatriz overcompensated. The jeep slammed into the other bank as she battled for control. The tires lost their grip and slid, but at the very last moment righted itself at the expense of more paintwork. By the time they emerged onto the next road crossing, Beatriz had them under control, and was able to steer up onto the tarmac without flipping the jeep.

She slowed their descent.

Lethe sank back into his seat, drained, shaking and anything but relaxed. But they were clear. There was no way Morais could follow them down that trail in one of the huge four by fours. He finally managed to relax his hold on the jeep's roll bar. His throat burned. He realised he'd been screaming most of the way down.

Cathy, on the other hand, was laughing.

Beatriz had a quiet smile on her face as she turned back to Lethe.

"Still alive, gringo?"

"You tell me. Start with who the fuck you are."

"My name is Beatriz Espinoza, currently on secondment from Peruvian Special Forces. I infiltrated the Shining Path forces five years ago."

"Five years without getting made?"

"Your friend, Mr Larkin, I think worked out I was more than a cook, but no one else."

"Noah?"

"Yes. My apologies, but I could not warn you what you were walking into."

He didn't say anything after that.

It took fifteen minutes before they reached the base of the mountain and drove over the bridge into Aguas Calientes.

Beatriz filled the silence. "I am going to drop you two off. You need to hide. The next train to Cusco leaves in just over an hour. There is a good chance they will expect you to be on it. But I'm going to try and sell the lie to Morais that you are still with me. If I can, I will lead her out of town."

"How? I thought there were no roads out of this town?"

"True," Beatriz said. "But you might have noticed I don't tend to need them." That earned a hoot of uncontrollable laughter from Cathy, as though it was the funniest thing she'd ever head. "Go. And make sure you are on that train."

"We will be."

"I just wasted five years of my life for you, Mister Lethe. Make sure it was worth it. Get the girl home. Call in your people. The dead deserve justice. Someone to speak for them."

"That's me," Lethe said, deadly serious. "Each and every last one of them will be reckoned for."

"Good. That is as it should be."

Beatriz dropped them off at bus park on the edge of town. The road ended there. She stopped beside a couple of tourists.

They looked nothing like Lethe and Cathy but would have to do.

She clambered out of the jeep.

"Cusco police," she said. "I need your backpacks, and I need you to get into the car." The couple looked confused for a moment, then they saw the gun she was holding discretely at her side. "No need to be afraid. I'll have you back here in a few minutes."

The backpacks came off quickly. Lethe and Cathy put them on. The two tourists got into the Jeep with Beatriz. She gave them a brisk wave and then she was off. Lethe couldn't let himself worry about the two tourists. Beatriz would look after them.

He checked his pack for anything useful. In the third pocket he found a mobile phone. There was no signal. Cathy checked her pack. Another phone, again no signal.

It didn't jibe.

He'd seen plenty of people using mobiles when they first arrived in town. They could be in a dead spot. They walked to the main street and melted into the throng of tourists. He checked the phone again. Nothing. Realising he was starving, he took the opportunity to buy food from a street vendor, something called *salchipapas*. What he received was basically hot dogs and chips. He ordered a bowl of *cau cau*, which he'd assumed was something beefy, given its bovine-sounding name. It turned out to be something slimy that defied identification. They stuck with the *salchipapas*. The next fifteen minutes were occupied inside one of the tourist shops browsing postcards and trinkets. Lethe bought them both sunglasses and hats, not that they'd fool anyone who looked closely enough.

Aguas Calientes was a small town dominated by the river.

Its sole purpose was to serve as a place to stay for visitors to Machu Picchu. Even so, it was oddly attractive, with one street leading up a steep hill to the hotels while another followed the train tracks. Restaurants and shops lined the railway track. There was no rhyme or reason to the various constructions, they had simply grown up organically, each one wildly different to the next. As with the buildings he'd seen in Lima, the upper storeys seemed unfinished.

Lethe took out his borrowed phone again. Still no signal. Looking around he saw a couple of others were having problems getting reception, but no one was panicking so word hadn't made it down the mountain of the slaughter. Yet.

"It's because no one can get reception. No one back at the site has been able to tell them what happened."

"You think Morais has sabotaged the cell tower?"

"Maybe. Even so it's a race. Word *is* going to spread. Unless they murder every last one of the people up there." He let that thought hang in the air for a moment.

"We've got to assume someone made it."

"Which means it'll be mayhem when the train pulls in."

They went with the flow of tourists. Halfway along the track, he saw a sign that raised his spirits for the first time in days.

Internet.

He set off towards it, practically dragging Cathy in his wake while he made a path, pushing his way towards the tiny café.

"Wait," she said.

"I need to contact Noah," he objected.

Then he saw what she'd seen.

A woman. Outside the café. She stood by the door, watching. He couldn't see a weapon. He didn't need to. He recognised her face from the plateau.

She was one of Morais's people.

Did that mean they knew they were here, or were they hedging their bets?

Lethe pulled the brim of the cap down to better cover his face, took Cathy's hand and crossed the tracks to the other side of the street, glancing back a couple of times as they continued on. Best he could tell, the woman hadn't made them.

He saw a second sign promising internet to patrons. Another familiar face lurked outside, leaving it out of bounds.

"Bastards," Lethe muttered. He was about to step out onto the tracks when a train whistle sounded. He stepped back another two paces just to be safe. The crowds parted as the old-fashioned diesel locomotive chugged through the town. Some of the vendors could have served their food through the passing windows.

The town was so small they were able to reach the station on the east side at the same time as the train.

No one moved to intercept them. He hadn't managed to make another of Morais's foot soldiers. Lethe dared to believe that maybe Beatriz had pulled it off.

He searched his borrowed backpack. There were two tickets for tomorrow afternoon. He wasn't about to let that stop him. "Come on," he said, handing one of them to Cathy. No one stopped them boarding. Rather than risk being challenged by someone whose seat they occupied, they opted to stand. He wanted to be moving before the guard reached them.

"We need to be in the middle of the train," Cathy said.

It made sense, the guard could come from either end, but he wouldn't start in the middle.

They made their way from one carriage to the next.

The carriage lurched, and with steel wheels squeaking on the rails it gradually pulled away.

A whistle blew.

Cathy didn't look happy.

She should have been happy.

They'd escaped.

"They still have my grandfather," she said. He'd forgotten. Even so, he was having a tough time mustering much sympathy for a Nazi, even if he was an old man now. There was no statute of limitations on the kind of horrors his kind had perpetrated. So if he died at the hands of Morais's thugs he wouldn't lose any sleep. It was different for her though. To her he was just Granddad.

"Or not," he said. Which didn't really help matters.

She nodded, lost in her own thoughts. She didn't want to think about what those two words meant, but there was no getting around the fact that the old man had outlived his usefulness, and he knew what people like Morais did to anyone they no longer needed. They'd both seen it first hand up on the mountain.

They rode on in silence. As the train reached the edge of the small town Lethe spared a thought for Beatriz. They both knew she was taking a one-way trip. She had blown her cover to save them, and had signed her own death warrant in the process.

The train lurched again.

Lethe staggered, stumbling into Cathy. They nearly fell. In the carriage behind them, bags dropped from overhead cages as the train stopped with an ear-piercing shriek.

"Ladies and gentlemen," a voice came from outside, amplified by a megaphone. "This is the police." It wasn't. It was Morais. "I apologise for the unscheduled stop. I promise you'll be on your way in just a moment, no need to worry. Please remain seated." She then spoke in Spanish, presumably repeating the same message, then switched back to English to add, "There are two people on board we need to talk to. Mr Lethe and Miss Dreschner, would you please make yourself known."

"Shit," Lethe said.

Cathy looked around for a way out- "Can we make a break for the trees?"

Lethe glanced out through the window. He couldn't see anybody out there. "Risky without knowing where Morais is." And even then, there was nowhere to run. All Morais needed to do was send her goons aboard to search the train. They were done.

"You're wasting time," the voice came again. "Beatriz is simply *dying* to see you."

There was confusion among the passengers. A couple stood up and leaned out of windows, trying to see what was going on. Others spoke in hushed voices.

"We have to go to her," Cathy whispered.

"No."

"What can we do?"

He thought for a moment about taking a tourist to use as a shield, but that wasn't his style.

Could they hide under the train or up on the roof?

"Nothing," he said eventually. "There's nothing we can do."

"Then I'll give myself up," Cathy said. "You stay here."

He shook his head. "Not happening."

"We're waiting," Morais called out, sounding thoroughly bored.

Lethe slammed a hand into the wall. A couple of the passengers eyed him suspiciously. He ignored them.

"Last chance, Mr Lethe," said Morais.

Two of the tourists in the carriage, big men with American flag bandanas, stood up and approached them.

"I think the police want to talk to you, dude," the bigger of the two said.

"If only they were the police," Lethe replied.

"Uh huh. Well buddy, they seem really interested in talking to you."

"They're Shining Path terrorists," Cathy said. "They want to kill us."

"Right. Of course they are," the other said.

Lethe laughed. "What? You think they should sound more *Middle Eastern*?"

"Jude, don't," Cathy warned.

He wasn't listening. "You've never heard of the Shining Path have you? They're a Peruvian terrorist group from the last century currently enjoying a resurgence. Think *Take That* with assault rifles."

"What the fuck are you talking about, man?"

"I'm educating a couple of ignorant Americans," Lethe said.

"What did you call us?"

"The word I used was ignorant," Lethe said. "If it helps, it means dumb as shit."

Cathy tried to pull him away. "What are you doing?"

"I'm hoping Jim Bob and Sue Ellen here will hand us over to the bad guys," Lethe said, loud enough for all to hear. "If we're going to give ourselves up, let's make sure these fine gentlemen *go with us* every step of the way."

He couldn't tell if she knew what he was trying to do.

"Happy to oblige, Boss," the first American said. "Wanna take a walk?"

"You asking?"

"No."

"Fine. Be gentle, pretty boy."

"Fucking idiot," the American muttered.

The man grabbed Lethe and frog marched him off the train. Cathy emerged two steps behind him. Lethe's heart was hammering. He was gambling with their lives and he had absolutely no cards left to play. Right now his life could be counted out in a couple of seconds.

The Americans escorted them the length of the train.

Passengers watched through the windows. Lethe made a point of smiling at them. He wanted them to see his face. He would have waved, but a two-hundred and fifty-pound bandana-wearing gorilla had hold of his arms. Sure enough, he spotted at least two tourists with their phones, videoing them through the windows. It might not be live streaming, but it was evidence that could be uploaded later. Wouldn't help him much, but might be enough for the old man to trigger a reckoning Lethe wouldn't be able to.

He kept on talking. "Smile for the cameras, boys."

The four of them reached the engine block. Morais was there with Guilherme and several of her Shining Path crew. They stood on the tracks. Morais had a gun pressed against the back of Beatriz's head. The undercover agent knelt at her feet.

"Ah, finally, Mr Lethe and Miss Dreschner. I was beginning to lose faith in you."

"Well look at that," Lethe said to their two impromptu captors. "A prisoner on her knees with a gun against her head. Still think you're turning us over to the cops?"

"Thank you, gentlemen," Morais said to the Americans. "We'll take it from here."

The American holding Cathy paused. "You don't mind, I'd kinda like to see some ID, ma'am?" he said to Morais.

She smiled sweetly. "Of course, why don't you come closer and have a look."

The big man took one step forward, straight into the bullet Morais fired towards his head. He went down without a word. Cathy screamed and recoiled, pulling away.

Lethe felt the hand on his arm loosen its grip.

"What did you think, Mr Lethe? Convince these fools we're terrorists and have them raise the alarm? That's a bit pathetic, isn't it?"

Lethe nodded, all bravado now gone. "You didn't have to kill him." He turned to the man beside him. "I'm so sorry."

Other people were getting off the train now, drawn out by the gunshot.

"This is on you, Jude. I wanted to do this quietly," Morais said.

"Strange idea of quiet you've got," he said, thinking of all those people back at Machu Picchu. He glanced back towards the train. Half a dozen travellers had disembarked and were making their way back to the town. More were climbing down from the carriage. Not all of them headed away from the commotion. Instead, out of some misguided sense of justice, they approached the dead American and the old woman on her knees. Maybe they thought they could help. Jude saw a couple who held their phones up, recording the action.

He wished they'd all just run away, because he knew what was going to happen next.

Morais gave the signal and her people started firing.

It only lasted a few seconds. Those seconds though were endless.

"I want you to remember that you did this, Mister Lethe. Their blood is on your hands."

He looked at the fallen with their discarded phones, lying in whorish sprawls where they'd gone down. They were all dead, and she was right, it was his fault.

Morais pressed the gun up against the back of Beatriz's head.

The woman didn't flinch. She looked at Lethe, met his eye, and then was gone as Morais pulled the trigger.

He saw the life leave her.

Lethe's legs betrayed him.

He dropped to the dirt.

The deaths of all these people... they were on him. His idiot scheme to involve the passengers, to complicate their surrender, to get his image out there on social media via people's phones so that Sir Charles might see it... this was all because of him.

The damage was done.

They were dead. There was no undoing that.

He felt Cathy put a hand on his shoulder.

"Stand up," she said. "We have to go."

He couldn't.

"You have to get up," she said. The inference being that if he didn't they'd kill her too. "Please."

Lethe tried to get to his feet, but the Shining Path men weren't willing to wait. They grabbed him and dragged him towards the waiting SUVs. He didn't fight them.

There was a newfound urgency to it all.

Lethe was only distantly aware of it. He noticed two of the terrorists collecting phones from the dead. There was going to be no last minute reprieve from an uploaded video.

Morais clambered into the front seat of a vehicle while Cathy, Lethe and Guilherme got into the back. He didn't recognise the driver.

He saw something in the sky. Black dots materialising. Cathy followed the direction of his stare as the distant buzzing sound intensified.

"Time to melt away." Morais said.

EIGHTEEN

Once again, Lethe found himself on the crumbling trail from Aguas Calientes to the Plateau.

He had never felt more defeated.

Less than three hours ago they'd boarded the train, free of this wretched place. How unbelievably, stupidly, naïve of him. There was no way out of this. He was an asset, a bargaining chip; Morais wasn't going to let him go without a fight.

The terrorist leader spoke to Guilherme in his native tongue. He laughed easily and offered something equally amusing in return. Lethe sat in brooding silence, wallowing in his own mistakes. He'd given up trying to escape. That way lay madness.

Morais took a call on her satellite phone.

He used the opportunity to talk to Guilherme.

"So," Lethe began, trying not to sound like he was embarking upon a fishing expedition. "The Shining Path, eh? I thought your lot had given up the ghost years ago."

Cathy glared at him for a moment, then returned to staring out of the window. Guilherme regarded Lethe warily, but the light of fanaticism burned bright in his eyes. Lethe had obviously hit on his favourite subject. The Brazilian man was more than happy to indulge him.

"No, no. They say were are gone, but that has only ever been propaganda. The lies of the government. They hide our uprising from the world. Or at least try. But in two years we have changed everything. Before, *el Sendero Luminoso* was little more than a few small groups scattered in the rural areas of the Andes, who spent their days growing cocaine and their nights smuggling it. That is what happens when a group lacks leaders, and ours were all dead or captured, so the rich man back in Lima was fool enough to think it was over." Lethe was sure for a moment he was about to say: *it had just begun*. He didn't. "Things changed for good with the defection of the General. Renzo Romero. He is a great man. A man of principle. Of honour. He could not stand by and see the corruption in the government and the army. You must understand the wealth gap in this country has been widening for years. The rich get richer while the poor live in squalor. General Romero was a beacon. He rallied huge numbers to his cause. In a year the Shining Path rose again, reclaiming all its former territory, Ayacucho, Apurímac, and Huancavelica. He was not content with that. Inside the next six months he added half of the Junín region."

They were interrupted by Morais. Her call was done. "That was Catalina at TV Peru. She says there's a video of Machu Picchu that's spreading everywhere. It doesn't show our prisoner's face." She smiled almost sweetly at Lethe then continued. "She's seen nothing from the train yet but she's monitoring YouTube, Instagram and other social media and will report if anything else comes up. Roberto will pick up the tourist who posted the footage of the incident."

Guilherme nodded.

It sounded so distant. Unreal. The incident. It wasn't an incident; it was a bloodbath.

Morais went back to her phone.

Lethe looked at Guilherme. "So Romero resurrected The Shining Path? I'm not seeing where Brazil fits into this?"

"That is because you do not see the world as the General does," Guilherme said. "Brazil was Romero's *grande conquista*. There was no way the poor regions of Peru could finance his plans, so he annexed the Madre de Dios region, on the border with Brazil. This area has always been the heart of trade in exotic animals to Brazil, and much of the illegal logging on the transoceanic highway. It is big money. Behind drugs and guns the trade in wildlife is the third largest black market in the world. Romero was a thorn in the Peruvian government's side. It was becoming more and more difficult for them to ignore him. Then he reached out to my organization. Six months ago the Communist Brazil Movement pledged our allegiance to The Shining Path. With Romero's help, we've taken control of over half the Acre region. Soon we will reach Rio Branco, as our reach grows so too does our wealth and influence. Romero believes it is inevitable that Bolivia will join our fight soon. Imagine a united South America? A new Union of Socialist Republics!"

Just what the world needs, thought Lethe, but knew better than to say it out loud.

"Why is nobody talking about this?" he asked instead. Truth be told, in the past few months he'd picked up a fair amount of background chatter on unofficial channels about conflicts and skirmishes all over south-east Peru, but this was organised resistance on a level those bulletin boards couldn't convey. What pissed him off was the fact that despite all the obvious evidence inevitably generated by such activities, national and international media weren't reporting it. The tourist dollar was obviously too valuable to risk.

"It is always about the money," Guilherme explained, confirming Lethe's unspoken assertion. "Governments in Peru and Brazil take handouts from foreign sources for promised investment and redevelopment schemes. Then there is the ultimate money laundering opportunity in the lead up to the World Cup, of course, with so much money coming and going through the bidding process and going to the corrupt. Unsurprisingly, no one wants to stop milking that cash cow, especially in the face of the coming civil war. So they hold silence. They hide the advances we make. They pretend we do not exist, but thanks to you the world will know us."

Lethe was about to ask just what the hell the Brazilian meant by that last statement, but they had reached the Plateau.

Armed soldiers waited for them.

The car stopped and they got out. Lethe noticed Morais was clutching something in her left hand. A short, portly man approached them, all smiles and nonchalance. He wore an open flak jacket, a camo cap and dark glasses. He broke out into laughter when Morais hugged him, his mirth raspy and smoke-abused.

"*Profesora! Dichosos los ojos que te ven!*"

The two conversed in Spanish before Morais finally turned to introduce her team.

"General Renzo Romero, *nuestro magnífico líder,* may I introduce Guilherme Rocha, our explosives expert." Guilherme nodded deferentially. "This pretty little thing is Cathy Dreschner, the granddaughter of our German friend in Lima." Cathy shook his hand reluctantly. "And this," Morais continued, "is Jude Lethe. He's the man who found both the door *and* the key."

General Romero clapped Lethe on the shoulder with some force. "Señor, we owe you a great debt. You have made all of this possible."

More fool me. "Glad to be of service," Lethe lied.

"Ha ha, my friend. The Professor has told me all about you and your... unique talents." He turned to the soldier standing beside Lethe, his rifle held ready. "What is all this? No need to push guns in his face. Where is he going to go, huh?" The general waved away the soldier, still laughing. What was it with tin pot dictators thinking they were the funniest men alive, always laughing at their own words even when there weren't any jokes? "Is he going to fly off the mountain? I don't think so." He turned the focus of his piercing eyes on Lethe, and asked the simplest question imaginable. "You are one of us now, no?"

No quips, no comebacks, no pithy insults. Like the Bee Gees said, it was all about staying alive. "Absolutely," Lethe said.

"Good! Good!" Romero nodded as though dozens of innocent people hadn't been gunned down by his people today. "Well, my new friend, we must wait a while longer to celebrate, but celebrate we will when our governments are on their knees. For now, we have work to do. You have the key, Camilla?"

"I do," Morais said, as though accepting his hand in a marriage of deadly convenience. She opened her hand to reveal an iron key. It was surprisingly large, with a long shaft and multiple prongs cut into the bit. At the head the iron formed a circle with an unmistakable icon within.

The swastika.

Lethe stared at the hateful object. The Nazi's had cocooned their treasure in a metal chamber, sealed it inside a mountain and hidden the key away within the ruins of the country's greatest national treasure. It had to be something valuable beyond imagining.

Romero handed the key to Lethe and motioned towards the iron door.

"It is only right that you should be the one to do the honours, Mister Lethe. After all, as Camilla so rightly says, you found both the door and the key."

Lethe didn't *want* the honour.

A beautiful image crossed his mind: the key sailing out into the nothing beyond the edge of the plateau, all of these bastards standing helplessly as it tumbled into the abyss.

He knew he'd never make it to the edge alive. So he did as he was told.

They had cleared away the last of the rock fragments blocking the door and swept away the debris. The incongruity of a giant metal door set into a roughly hewn alcove in the side of the mountain was almost like an illustration from a children's book. The key in his hand was real enough though. He pushed it into the keyhole, hoping against hope that it wouldn't fit or that it might sheer in two as he tried to turn it. The pins caught, he heard them falling into place with some resistance, rust and age tightening the mechanism. As the key completed a full revolution a smaller door within the door opened up. Beyond lay darkness.

Lethe wasn't going to be first to cross the threshold. He'd seen Indiana Jones.

Soldiers dispensed hard hats with flashlights attached to the rim. The general declined, unwilling to take off his camo cap. Lethe took one and turned the torch on. He wasn't about to rely on anyone else for light in there.

Morais was first in, followed by two soldiers.

The general ushered Lethe and Cathy forward. They stepped into the darkness together.

Their helmet lights revealed a long passageway; longer than he'd expected from the GPR scans. There were various darker recesses along its length. Doors, he presumed.

Morais reached the first and opened it.

Living quarters.

This lost city wasn't just some treasure trove; an entire military base had been carved out of the mountain. "Incan city my arse," Lethe grumbled.

"I can't believe my grandfather built this," Cathy's voice carried in the gloom, echoing off the metal walls. Lethe kept quiet after that.

They continued down the tunnel, beams of light leading the way.

The air was old. Stale.

The sheer scale of the excavation was immense. At the end of the passage a lift shaft with a spiral staircase built around it led downwards. The lift had no power; whatever generator used to fuel it rusted beyond repair. Morais led them down the stairs. Their boots clanged off the metal steps as they descended. The curves snaked around the wire cage of the lift shaft again and again. Below, the shaft opened up into a vast subterranean cavern. They continued their descent. The beams from their torches weren't strong enough to penetrate the darkness more than fifteen or twenty feet. There was no indication the chamber ever ended. And still they climbed down. The builders must have hollowed out more than half of the mountain; at least that was how it felt to Lethe, but eventually they came to the bottom of the iron stairs.

They stepped off onto a metal gangway.

Morais took a more powerful torch from her belt and turned it on.

They were confronted by a breath-taking sight. The cavern was impossibly huge. Hundreds of metres of pipes stretched high above them in all directions, following a continuous circuit winding around itself and then spreading out, making maximum use of the available space. She shone her light upwards, revealing more pipework alongside access gantries and more staircases. It looked like the insides of an old German U-Boat, Lethe realised.

They traversed the walkway. Lethe looked over the edge and immediately wished he hadn't. The beam from his torch wasn't strong enough to reach the ground. As he moved his head back and forth he saw the bulk of several silver vats. Best he could tell they took up the entire cavern floor. Which meant there were hundreds of them, hundreds upon hundreds, stretching far beyond the range of his light.

He focussed on his feet, thinking.

This level contained at least four separate rooms, all constructed with their own walls and roofs, like porta cabins.

Morais led them into the first metal room. An impressive, if primitive array of control dials and read-out screens filled the room. Whatever the purpose of this hidden facility, this was obviously its unbeating heart. Curiosity drove Lethe to examine the huge bank of instrumentation more closely. He recognised some if not all of the controls, they weren't so different to the type found in old hydro-electric power plants. Was that what this was? It seemed... unlikely. A thick patina of dust covered everything. He brushed some of it off so he could read the instruments. They were all in German or Spanish, but some words, including "Voltage" didn't need any translation.

"A generator?" Lethe wondered. "Water driven, at a guess."

"Is that what all the pipes are for?" Cathy asked.

"My guess is they're designed to collect the rainwater flowing down the mountain and channel it through the turbines to generate power."

Morais said nothing.

They left the room.

The second chamber was full of ancient banks of computers, huge bulky boxes with tape reels attached behind glass windows. There was more processing power in his mobile phone. In the centre of the room he saw a single desk. There were papers stacked neatly beside an old Royal pearl-keyed typewriter. The computer banks lined all four walls. They were dominated by dials and knobs, meters and levers. There must have been a hundred of them in this one room.

He'd assumed the silver vats were some sort of battery array, but now he wasn't so sure.

Perhaps the next room was a laboratory.

All manner of paraphernalia covered the workbenches. He saw an impressive variety of mechanical parts, beakers and vials, pipets and more chemistry equipment. There were calibrators and measuring devices, too. He had no idea what they'd been doing in this place, but it looked like they had stopped in a hurry. Desk after desk piled high with pieces of archaic technology seemingly abandoned mid-experiment. Sixty years ago this stuff would have been cutting-edge technology.

Morais's powerful torch beam settled on a large object at the far end of the room.

Additional beams of converged on it, as though it were the Holy Grail. The lights came together to reveal more and more of its shape. Even so, it was difficult to make out exactly what it was because a sheet of glass between them and the object reflecting much of the light.

Lethe walked towards the glass.

The bulk of it was a large cylindrical tank, like a barrel-shaped metal tube. It tapered to a thinner tube at one end before expanding at the tail into a fan-like attachment with stabilizing fins.

It was a bomb. And not just *any* bomb. The shape of the device was distinctive and deeply familiar. It was ingrained on the psyche.

This was *Little Boy*.

Not the *actual* Little Boy; the original bomb had vaporised over Hiroshima in 1945, taking an entire city and sixty thousand people with it. But here it was: the world's first atomic bomb, recreated by Nazis within a secret base hidden inside a Peruvian mountain. He was looking at the revenge fantasies of those refugee Nazi officers who had never intended the war to end.

He didn't have words.

Slowly, he began to discern slight differences from the iconic design, but they were slight. These men—Cathy's grandfather among them—had succeeded in doing what Nazi Germany had failed to do during the war: they had built a nuclear weapon.

Being in the presence of such awesome destructive power was truly humbling. It made little difference that the bomb was crude by modern standards. Its killing power was beyond imagining. He was in the presence of one of humanity's most impressive accomplishments, and its worst.

General Romero approached the glass, placing his hands on it and staring at the device.

"This is better than gold, don't you think?" he asked Lethe.

Lethe had no answer to that.

The general said something in Spanish. Lethe wasn't listening. He was looking at the end of the world as he knew it.

Beyond the first bomb there lay another, and two more besides.

"*A bolada,*" said Morais.

NINETEEN

Noah couldn't feel his arms.

His shoulders and back were a different matter.

He could *more* than feel them.

With his wrists behind his back, hauled painfully by the chain, his forced crouch could only alleviate so much of the discomfort. He hadn't slept. The pain wasn't enough to make him pass out, either.

He was desperately thirsty.

But this was good.

They weren't beating him.

No one was peeling the skin away from his hands with hot piano wire. No one was crushing his skull in a vice.

But that didn't mean he wasn't being tortured. This was mind games. The worst, most effective weapon in his enemy's arsenal? That he knew Lethe was out there on his own. Lethe wasn't made for this. He had his own unique skillset. Noah was banking on the fact that Lethe was resourceful. He might not be physically tough, but the kid could think on his feet. He'd get a message out to the old man by hook or by crook—most likely crook given the nature of this tin pot regime—and any minute now Frost and Koni would drop in to say *hola*.

A commotion outside the door had Noah, for one glorious moment, believing the cavalry had arrived.

They hadn't.

He was still alone here.

"*Lo encontraron!*" someone said. "*Lo encontraron!*"

Good news, Noah assumed, given the excitement.

There weren't many causes for excitement he could think of, beyond Lethe finding gold up in them there hills. It didn't change things for him, even if they were nearing their end game. It just made matters more pressing. His date with a bullet was getting closer. And as much as he liked a decent fuck, he wasn't about to turn up for that particular blind date.

He gritted his teeth and stretched a leg, ignoring the shooting pains that travelled down his spine in the process. He needed to get the blood flowing again. He was only going to get one shot at getting out of the shit.

But he needed to keep it hurting, too. The pain was going to be the only thing that might make what he was about to do more bearable.

He angled his body, trying to manoeuvre his wrists under his arse.

He was going to need to dislocate his shoulder to do that.

Tearing his rotator cuffs might make it more difficult to beat Carlos to death with his bare hands, but Noah was willing to try.

No pain no gain.

He regulated his breathing, deep and slow followed by fast and shallow until he was light-headed, then deep and slow again. Then he pulled himself forward as far as he could go, straining against the chains, trying to tip his body forward so that his weight and gravity would come together in one beautifully agonising moment and he would in effect somersault through his bound arms and end up with his hands chained above his head. Not that he was sure tearing his shoulders out of joint would benefit him in the long run. But he had to do *something*. He couldn't just sit here and wait to die. That wasn't him. He was the stupid, impetuous one. That was what kept him alive.

He pushed himself forward into the somersault.

The pain in his shoulders soared.

He blacked out.

TWENTY

Lethe placed his hand on the bomb's shell.

He *almost* convinced himself the metal casing was vibrating. Just slightly. Simmering. Alive. It wasn't. The device was inert. Guilherme swept the room with a Geiger counter. The reading came back safe. The bombs might have been silent for decades, but they were anything but powerless.

"I don't—" Cathy started to ask, but there were too many questions in her head for them to come out. Lethe couldn't imagine how she must be feeling, to discover that dear old granddaddy had made four nukes... "I knew they were looking for a weapon... but I never imagined... not in my wildest dreams."

"A weapon capable of levelling a city the size of Hiroshima," he said. He didn't need to say anything more.

Morais opened one of four crates piled up on one of the nearby workbenches. She unpacked various items, including bags filled with some kind of powder and three wooden pegs. The pegs had one end painted green. There were three matching red-topped pegs protruding from the bomb's housing. It didn't take a genius to work out that switching the green for the red would prime the bomb.

"They can't still be in working order, surely," Cathy said, a note of hope in her voice. "The innards must have decayed over the last sixty years."

Lethe crouched down to get a better look underneath the bomb. It was supported by a wooden cradle, raised off the floor by three feet so that every curve was accessible. "The detonator, maybe, but the uranium in these things will last for thousands of years. I can't see any damage to the casing, so assuming they *ever* worked, I'd be willing to bet—" he was about to say his life, but held that little nugget back. "—they still pack a hell of a punch."

Guilherme took a screwdriver to the tail section of the bomb he was examining, opening it up. He unlatched the fins and swung them away to reveal an opening.

He shone a torch inside.

The glare from the beam transformed his face through the shadows into a death's head skull for just a moment. The illusion was fleeting, but perfect. "The firing mechanism's still good. All we need to do is load the bags of cordite, replace the pins and set the timer."

Morais joined him. She nodded, running her hand almost tenderly across the metal shell. "We'll replace the trigger anyway. Is the uranium intact?"

"Can't imagine anyone's been down here to disturb it," he said. "We're looking at precision engineered quality components. I don't see any warping or corrosion."

"Thanks to you, Mister Lethe, the Shining Path has just turned Peru into a world power."

Behind her, the general chuckled his mirthless rasp of a laugh. "Now, now, Camilla, my dear, don't tell them all our plans. I would hate to have to kill our new friends."

"These are *nuclear* weapons," Lethe objected, trying to wrap his head around their casual disregard for life. It didn't matter that he'd seen them murder countless tourists in cold blood, the numbers, the sheer scale of killing these things were capable of, it was hard to grasp and impossible to imagine actually deploying them. "You can't…"

"Oh, I assure you, we *can*." Morais told him. "And will. We are fighting for people all over this continent who have *nothing*. For decades they have had nothing. Nobody was helping the ignored before us. They were simply left to die. Poverty worsens all around us while the rich bleed this country dry. With these bombs we will tear down the corrupt governments and slaughter the greedy pigs. It is time that my people had hope."

"Enough, Professor," Romero warned quietly. "This is neither the time or place for lectures."

Morais said nothing. It was the first glimpse of the professor's soul Lethe had witnessed in all his time in captivity.

"Now, we have work to do," Romero said. "Guilherme, how long will it take you to replace the trigger mechanisms?"

The explosives man shrugged noncommittally.

"It'll take time."

"Do it here. Then we shall move them. Camilla, take our guests back to the surface. We don't require them down here. Call in the choppers so that they are in place when Guilherme is done."

She nodded.

A silent Morais led Lethe and Cathy back to the gangway. Two soldiers followed behind. Passing under the immense network of pipes, Cathy asked the question that had been weighing on her mind since the nature of this place had been revealed. "Did my grandfather build this?"

Morais told her, "In '46, your grandfather was in Argentina. He fled Germany along with the other cowards and war criminals too frightened to own what they had done. They learned of a hollow mountain in Peru, having intercepted the explorer who discovered it. They murdered him before he could tell the world of his incredible find. A lost city hollowed away inside the earth."

They neared the end of the gangway.

Two men were attempting to connect a generator to the lift, which would make transporting the bombs to the surface easier.

They took the iron stairs.

"Before the war, Herr Dreschner designed and built hydro-electric power plants in Europe. He used his skills to build one here inside the mountain, and as you can see, his design was highly efficient for its day. Indeed, it was capable of generating enough power for the Nazis to pursue their real goal."

"Nuclear vengeance," Lethe said.

"Precisely," Morais replied. The climb took its toll on Lethe but didn't seem to affect the older woman. "By that time they were aware America had the bomb. Remember these were the days of espionage and the Cold War. There were sympathisers in all ranks. They made contact with a group who had access to Los Alamos Laboratory's original designs for Little Boy, and, crucially, details of the centrifuges used to enrich uranium.

"Your grandfather was a brilliant engineer. He oversaw the construction of the power plant and the enrichment facility, and he was the man who built the actual bombs from those blueprints. He made them a reality."

"How many Nazis worked here?" Lethe asked, expecting the answer to be fifty or a hundred.

She said, "Just five."

"How could five men build all this?"

"This, everything you see here, is just half of the operation. They brought looted gold with them and they paid for raw materials and workers to construct this place. It wasn't a secret. All those legends of Nazi Gold, well this is where it went, into funding the small army needed to build this place. They laid the road we took to get here. They even constructed a temporary village to house all the workers. They had a similar operation down south at the Macusani Plateau, but that was a uranium mine not a weapons facility. The ore was shipped here to be enriched using the centrifuges. It took a decade before Herr Dreschner had enough enriched uranium to build his bombs."

"After all that, why didn't he use them?" Cathy asked.

"That is a question you should ask him yourself," Morais said as they reached the top of the stairs. She led them back towards the sunlight at the far end of the passageway.

More of Romero's soldiers hurried past carrying lighting, generators and other equipment.

"He might claim some form of conscience, an awakening after all those years, but I don't believe he ever had the chance to use them. The operation was compromised while Herr Dreschner waited for a visit from the most senior Nazi exile in South America. His superior never made it here. He was captured and interrogated before being shipped back to The Hague to stand trial for his crimes. Herr Dreschner had no way of knowing if he had been betrayed, and in panic buried the entrance to this place. Explosives were used to trigger an artificial mudslide which wiped out the makeshift village. The labourers were killed. Likewise, the miners at the Macusani Plateau were killed in a tunnel collapse. It was all very expedient. Herr Dreschner and his friends fled to Brazil. You know the rest," she said to Cathy. "It is your story after all."

Rather than take them outside, Morais pushed them through the door into one of the dormitory rooms.

The door closed and Cathy and Lethe were alone.

A quick search failed to turn up anything of use so they sat down on bunks opposite each other.

"Is it hard to enrich uranium?" Cathy asked him.

"Incredibly. All those vats lining the floor of the cavern, those are centrifuges. They're used to separate uranium 238 from U-235. You need mostly U-235 to build a bomb, and natural uranium is mostly U-238." Which, he could tell meant nothing to her.

"Why are there so many of them?"

"It's a tedious process. Each centrifuge spins and separates the isotopes, but you need a huge chain of them to refine enough U-235 to build a bomb."

"Before today," she said, "Peru wasn't a nuclear power." She didn't need to say what would happen after today. The darkness made it all too easy to imagine.

TWENTY ONE

The battery on Lethe's helmet lamp died. With it went the last of the light.

Cathy was sleeping. She'd turned her lamp off to preserve the battery. He thought about waking her, but he wasn't afraid of the dark. Yet. He was sure that would come.

Time crawled through the darkness.

He tried to occupy his mind with a mathematical puzzle to solve, running the numbers in his head over and over.

Overhead lights flickered.

For a moment he thought he was having a fit, that a blood vessel had burst in his brain. Then the lights came on.

He saw Cathy blink herself awake.

"What happens now?" she asked.

"A show of power," Lethe said. He'd been thinking about what that might entail for most of the time she'd been asleep. That was the equation he'd been calculating; the various population densities of cities within a five-hundred-mile radius, the payload of the bomb, the casualties, blast zone radius and fallout potential. None of the numbers were reassuring.

No government would capitulate to terrorists based on threats alone, but the fallout of a vaporised city? That would do it.

"We're still alive because Morais needs us for something." Lethe stopped himself from saying any more. Just because Cathy was locked up with him didn't mean she was a prisoner. She'd already admitted to playing him once. What was to say she wasn't doing it again?

He needed to stop assuming she was on his side.

"I think we should get some sleep," he suggested. He could smell the dust on the lights burning. Lethe examined the simple bulbs with their metal shades. Very functional. Very fifties. Dust covered everything, but not as much as he'd expected, even if it was enough to smell bad in the heat of the overhead lights.

If he ever did make it home, he'd never leave Nonesuch again.

TWENTY TWO

Romero's people worked through the night.

The lift was now in service.

The doors opened. Lethe saw soldiers push a large crate on wheels out into the corridor. Lethe was forced to press up against the wall to let them pass. It didn't take a nuclear physicist to know what was inside the box.

"That one's going to Rio," Morais said, coming up behind them. "The next is destined for Lima. Of course, you'll be involved in deploying it."

"What on Earth could possibly make you think I'd help you?" he said.

"Do I need to shoot her to bring you into line?" she replied, pointing at Cathy.

"Shoot her you lose your leverage over me. Doesn't seem like the best plan if you ask me."

"Your role isn't up for debate. Follow me now."

She ushered them into the lift. She drew the iron gate closed behind them. Morais pressed the only button on the dial and machinery creaked into life.

"You know I don't want to die. I know I don't want to die. I don't particularly want Cathy to die, or any of the thousands of people who might be caught in the fallout from a bomb, so if you seriously think I'm going to help you murder them, hundreds of thousands of innocent people... the numbers don't add up. I won't do it. I'll die first if that's what it takes."

"Mr Lethe," Morais said. "I don't care how you justify it to yourself. I don't care for your personal morality. You *are* going help us. Maybe you're right, shooting Miss Dreschner in the head won't motivate you, but rest assured, I will find some other way motivate you."

An unsettling truth descended on Lethe as the lift reached the bottom of the shaft.

"You've been lying all along, haven't you? This was never about helping you find the door. I'm the fall guy, aren't I?"

"Well, well, well," Morais chuckled, leading them out and along the gangway. "The penny drops. Now, I'm more than happy to admit you have had your uses, and almost certainly located the entrance faster than we might have done without you, but yes, *this* is why I asked Charles for your help. Not that I could tell him the real reason."

"He's going to be pissed if you blow me up."

"He'll forgive me. It wouldn't be the first time. He's always so noble, so committed to preserving the status quo." Lethe said nothing. "It's men like him, men with true power, who keep the world ticking over, preventing global collapse." She chuckled. "But and the end of the day, he'll do pretty much *anything* for me. That's the way the world works."

"You must have sold him one fuck of a lie for him to trust you."

"Guilt is a powerful motivator. Regret even more so. You know him. He possesses a very misguided sense of duty. But it is good to know that when I whistle he still comes running."

The old man had never mentioned her, but that didn't necessarily mean anything. Sir Charles was an intensely private person. His life was a closed book. But there was no doubting that her hold over him was absolute however she maintained it. If it was love, then that flame still burned strong enough to blind him to her true nature.

They reached a room beyond the bomb lab. Morais opened the door. Lethe hadn't been in here before. He was greeted by a scene lifted straight from a Nazi war film.

Wood panelling lined the walls of the large office. Two were adorned with Nazi imagery. Directly opposite the doors hung the Reichsadler eagle atop a wreath with a swastika. The iconography was repeated throughout the room. At one end was a wide desk and at the other an area with more comfortable wingback leather chairs, gathered around a presumably fake fireplace. In the middle of the room was a tabletop with a map of the world embossed onto it. A portrait of Hitler had fallen from the wall behind the desk. Nobody had bothered to rehang it. Aside from this one aberration, the office was perfectly preserved. Wall mounted lamps offered subdued light at regular intervals, and a standard lamp stood in each of the four corners.

Two armed guards stood either side of the entrance.

Romero was already in the room, hunched over the tactical map.

He glanced up at them.

"Camilla, how are things progressing?"

"One bomb is already on the surface. The helicopter is en route."

"And the detonators?"

"Two switched to remote triggers, linked to my cell phone. Guilherme is working on the third now."

"Good. Very good. Once all the devices are in situ we can bury this place. Although, there is something appealing about the grandeur of it all," he looked at the fallen image of the

Führer. "And its history. This map is really quite fascinating. The world was a very different place sixty years ago. Look at the Soviet Union, still so strong on this map, still united."

Morais moved over to the tactical table as Romero unfolded a more up-to-date map of South America.

"We already hold Arequipa, when Rio and Lima fall power will naturally shift into our hands. Peru will be free of the shackles of foreign investment and free to join with Brazil to form the foundation of a powerful union that will in time become a superpower. We will hold two nuclear weapons and will be able to replicate and refine what we've discovered right here. Imagine it, the day when Argentina and Chile join our union. Together we could be so much stronger than any nation state."

Lethe stared at him. "Eight and a half million people live in Lima. Six and a half million live in Rio. You're willing to murder them to see your dream realised? Don't you see how *sick* that is?"

"Lima is a doomed city," Romero said. "It rests on a fault line and could crumble at any moment. We would simply be speeding up its inevitable collapse."

"Fifteen million people," Lethe said.

"You are failing to see the bigger picture, Mister Lethe," said Morais. "Nothing changes without bloodshed. That is a fact of life. Without the bombs dropped on Hiroshima and Nagasaki the war could well have continued for years. Millions more might have died for every year the conflict dragged on if not for the deaths of those two hundred thousand poor souls. And from those radioactive ashes Japan rebuilt itself into a mighty nation. The same could be true for Peru. Think of this as a catalyst. Sometimes sacrifice is necessary. It is the nature of change."

"Necessary evil? Is that your excuse?"

"We are agents of change," Morais answered. "Millions of people live in poverty throughout South America. Our governments have had decades of growth and rich foreign investment to make them fat while they have done *nothing* for our people. We intend to make history happen, one way or another."

"This is insane," Lethe said. "You do know that, don't you? It won't work. It can't."

Morais locked eyes with him. "Do you have any real understanding of how many people have died because of what you and your team have done? Can you always be sure what you are told to do is morally right? The greater good, *necessary* evil. Your kind don't ask, you just obey. You hide behind your computers and your monitors, and change lives and destroy careers and commit murder every day. Do you ever question your orders? Do you ever wonder if it's the right thing to do when you tell Mr Larkin which target to gun down? Do you ever stop to ask if they deserve to die? Or do you just accept your orders?"

"It's not the same, and you know it," Lethe said, trying not to let himself be goaded by a terrorist.

"That's right, because you still believe you are one of the good guys," Morais mocked.

"I don't care what you think, Sir Charles is a *good* man," Lethe said.

"But have you ever turned your skills against him? Have you ever investigated his past? I guarantee you would be horrified by your discoveries. He is not what he seems to be. When you know the truth perhaps you will turn to your friend Ronan Frost and ask him to murder Charles for you?"

"I don't know what you're smoking, but I want some of it," Lethe said.

"You are so certain. It is really quite touching, but it is very, very naïve. You live such a sheltered life in Charles's mansion, protected from the outside world where real soldiers fight and die for causes they believe in. I know how you think, Mister Lethe. You put a distance between yourself and the crimes of your team, but there is blood on your hands."

Lethe couldn't speak.

He refused to show weakness to these people but Morais was getting under his skin and pissing him off.

Through sheer force of will, Lethe stayed silent.

He kept his eyes downcast.

He wanted them to think they had broken him.

He wanted them to believe he would help them. That the fight had left him.

"In the end, it doesn't matter," Morais said, "You're going to help us place these bombs, we both know it, because you are a coward."

"You know me so well," Lethe said, channelling his inner Noah.

TWENTY THREE

"I don't need the script. You really haven't got my voice down."

Carlos moved his face to within inches of Noah's. He could smell the ingredients of his last three meals. Curiously, that did nothing to fuel his hunger.

"You will read the script."

"Are you really that fucking stupid? If I read the *same* script the old man will know something's wrong. I'm going off script, and that's exactly what you'd want if you had half a brain."

Carlos didn't appreciate Noah's tone, and Noah didn't give a shit. He wasn't into the touchy feely crap. He was buying time. Stalling. Each hard earned minute gave his arms more time to recover their strength. Given long enough they might stop being ornaments. He flexed, working the muscles.

Noah stared at Carlos's face.

Half an inch closer and he'd be within biting distance.

He could tear the man's face off. It wouldn't be his first time.

As though reading his mind, Carlos backed off. "Then I will write you a new script," he said.

"I'll improvise. It'll be more convincing."

"I don't trust you," Carlos said.

"Christ, we don't have fucking safe words. Okay, how about this? You point your penis enhancer at my head and if I say anything you don't like, pull the trigger."

Carlos considered this, then nodded. "Okay, yes," he said at last. "I look forward to shooting you when you say something I don't like. *Entiendes?*"

"I have no idea what that means, but sure."

Carlos connected the call.

He stood off camera, with the pistol aimed at Noah's head.

"Noah, is that you?"

"In the flesh."

"Are you all right? Mister Lethe? I've seen coverage of the massacre at Machu Picchu."

"Not guilty. Look, you're not going to want to hear this, boss, but the trail's gone cold here. I think I'm going back to the mountains to meet up with Jude. Make sure he's okay."

"I think that's for the best. And remind him of the importance of regular contact. We have these protocols for a reason."

"Will do. Stay Frosty."

The old man paused, barely a nanosecond's stumble, but still longer than Noah would have liked. To his credit he covered it well, making up some bullshit.

"I nearly forgot. We found some information that might be of use to you out there. Maxwell's been helping me, because I cannot work these confounded machines of Lethe's to save my life. Check your inbox."

"Will do."

"Goodbye, Mister Larkin."

And with that the call ended.

Noah regarded Carlos impassively; he didn't know how much the other man knew about the team, but the old man had caught his reference to Frost. It wasn't the smoothest SOS, and the phrase quite literally meant *don't* send Frost, make him stay. But he was improvising.

"Okay, back to your cell."

"Hold on,"

"What is it now?"

"I'm busting for a piss. You got a bucket or something?"

Carlos nodded to one of his men who headed upstairs.

"Thank you. I'll be sure to give you a 5-star review on Yelp when I get home."

"You think you're going home?"

TWENTY FOUR

Be fearful what you wish for.

It was a monkey's paw moment. He was finally in front of a computer. But, if he did what they wanted he'd be triggering a catastrophic event, delivering loss of life on a massive scale.

On the other side of the desk, Morais stared at her own laptop.

"Just a reminder, Mister Lethe," she said, "Every keystroke you make, I'll be watching you, mirrored here on my screen." Everything he did was visible to her. Everything he typed, every window he opened, every site he visited, she would see it too.

"Oh, can't you see," he half sung. "You belong—"

"You really don't have the voice for it," Morais said.

He had a problem.

Theoretically he could still use the connection to raise the alarm in any number of ways. The first, and glaringly obvious one would be sending a cry for help back to Nonesuch. Ten seconds, maybe less, and he could bring the full force of Ogmios's fist down on these fuckers. It was tempting. The old man wasn't the most techno-savvy though, so he'd have a better chance with either Frost or Koni.

Ten seconds.

But those ten seconds would kill Cathy.

The phrase was collateral damage, but the reality of it, looking the woman in the eye, was so much more concrete than that. It was intimate. Real. Whereas someone like Noah would just dehumanise it to make the death of one person acceptable. To Lethe, sacrificing her wasn't acceptable. The Canadian sat in a plastic chair, hands in her lap and her head bowed. Morais's gun was on the table beside her computer, eight inches from her right hand. The threat was implicit. One wrong keystroke or touchpad swipe and goodbye.

Option two was alerting the Peruvian authorities.

The problem was getting them to take him seriously. And, again, how to do it without Morais spotting his sleight of hand and redecorating the walls with Cathy's brains?

"Any time you like, Mister Lethe," Morais said.

His first task, disable security at the *Torre Del Centro Cívico de Lima*, an office building in the heart of the city. It was the highest structure within range of the Parliamentary Palace at the Plaza de Armas. Detonating the bomb at an altitude of one hundred feet or more above the ground would ensure the maximum impact in the widest blast zone short of dropping it out of a plane and raining radioactive debris down from the heavens. He wasn't surprised that Romero's people weren't flying it in; with the Shining Path's politicised ultimatum being delivered first, the armed forces would almost certainly adopt a shoot on sight policy for hostile incursions. This way they primed the bomb in advance of making their threats.

Lethe opened a connection to the building's security system.

Most computer systems weren't sandboxed. It was lazy security, more often than not instead of running multiple network solutions they worried about blunt force attacks and firewalls and basic security like rotating passwords when it concerned corporate espionage, not building maintenance.

In ideal circumstances he'd have the luxury of time to run a script to ferret out a potential target account, breach through poor user practices rather than his own hacking protocols, but he didn't have time. Or his scripts, for that matter. He *could* write a new routine under Morais's suspicious eye, but he'd be worrying that every other line of code would trigger her itchy finger. It took all of two minutes to confirm that Cyber Security in Peru was, at best, lax.

He set to work rooting the system.

All he needed was administrative access, so the first step was identifying accounts with that clearance. In this instance it was every single account registered on the network. "I need to write a short piece of code. You aren't going to understand what it means. You need to trust me."

"Do it," she said. "You have no idea what languages I understand."

He opened up a Linux terminal and crafted a short script to run through the gamut of alphanumeric passwords drawing on words from an online dictionary database, that would hit every single account in the system until it bludgeoned one into submission. It wasn't pretty, but it was effective. Back home it would have set every alarm bell ringing and brought the house crashing down on him. Here, it opened doors.

"I'm in," he said. "From here I can access the building layout, various maintenance systems, that sort of stuff. I'm not on the corporate side, but I assume that's not what you're after?"

"A fair assumption. Are you familiar with the system?"

"Not particularly, but one back end is much like another, even if everything is in Spanish. I'll find my way through. It looks like they're in the process of adding more sophisticated systems sitting on top of the older core so I'll need to be careful."

Morais nodded. "Disable the alarms on the loading dock entrance at the back of the building. Access security camera footage and manipulate it to show a loop that doesn't reveal the movements of my people."

"Easy enough," Lethe said. He wasn't bragging. This was what he did, and like the old Bond song said, nobody did it better. He called up the building schematics, pinpointing camera locations and security locks. Without a GUI everything was run through the command line interface, which meant he was hammering out commands faster than the cursor lag could cope with. He was lucky. If the back end had been any more antiquated he would have been locked out. There were warehouses still running their security on old Commodore 64s, this at least was some sort of Linux kernel. It made a difference. His encryption key sliced through the system's inner defences.

He triggered the door release remotely.

Through the cameras he watched two guards near the loading dock's cargo doors. They were deep in conversation.

Lethe ran another command line code.

Simultaneously both men on the screen checked their cell phones, which vibrated with the alert Lethe just initiated. There was split second of indecision, then they were moving: running towards the security office on the second floor. It would buy a couple of minutes at most. His next command line code intercepted the feed from the cameras, replacing the image on the monitors at the front desk with a single second of looped video captured just as the men left the shot. Done, he piggybacked another server that still received the live video feed and brought it up in a separate window.

Morais put on a headset and began issuing orders to her team.

Thirty seconds later Lethe saw the shadow of a truck pulling up in front of the cargo doors.

He'd given himself his own set of mission objectives to run counter to Morais's instructions. There was some overlap; he would watch out for guards, manipulate the building's security, and help the team exfiltrate without the loss of life, but that was where their interests diverged.

"Can I talk directly to the team?"

Morais nodded. There was a second headset beside his monitor. He put it on. "This is Lethe. Who am I speaking to?"

"Carlos," a familiar voice said. Lethe went cold. Carlos had left with Noah. Now Carlos was here. What did that mean for Noah? Alive? Dead? He couldn't let himself think about that.

"I won't ask you how Noah's doing. You've got a guard heading your way. Thirty seconds out. Coming from the offices at the back of the bay."

Lethe and Morais watched the three men flatten themselves against a wall, waiting for the unsuspecting guard.

"Behind you is a door to a janitor's cupboard," said Lethe. "I suggest you use it."

Carlos tried the handle and the door opened.

Lethe watched the Shining Path men step inside. The door closed just as the guard turned the corner. Lethe watched him as he scanned the cargo bay, then walk on. When he was out of sight, Lethe told Carlos "You're clear."

The three men emerged from hiding.

Four more people entered, pushing a large crate on wheels. There was writing on the crate but because of the poor resolution on the cameras he couldn't read it. No doubt it said "Fuck You Lima" or some such on it.

"Thank you, Jude," said Carlos. He might have been talking to an old friend. The feeling wasn't mutual.

"Anything for you, good buddy," he lied. "Retrace the guard's footsteps, you'll find a service elevator just around the corner. I'm disabling those cameras now."

The terrorists moved swiftly, considering they were transporting a nuclear bomb in a crate. As they waited for the lift to arrive at the ground floor, something occurred to Lethe, so he checked more out of idle curiosity than expectation. According to the inspection log the last entry was over five years old. It recorded various running repairs, including a note on the condition of the cabling within the elevator shaft. There was nothing in the service records to suggest the cabling had been replaced.

He debated holding his tongue.

Morais was watching him. She'd seen everything he'd seen.

"Don't board the lift," he said. "Not with the bomb. The payload's too heavy. The cabling is worn. There's no guarantee it'll hold. Send up three of your team, then send the cargo on its own."

"No," Carlos said. "I'm not letting it out of my sight."

"It's your life buddy. If you plunge to your death in the lift shaft don't come running to me."

"Dead men don't run, Mr Lethe," Carlos said, dryly.

"Indeed."

Morais weighed him up, trying to decide if Lethe was manoeuvring her men into a trap.

Lethe flashed her a smile.

He covered his mike and said, "You're going to have to trust me, Prof." He looked pointedly at the gun. "I don't have any romantic ideas about suicide."

Morais nodded.

Carlos sent three of his men up to the top floor in the service elevator. Lethe watching the Brazilian waiting impatiently at the bottom as the lift made its agonizingly slow return.

When it finally arrived, Carlos and his remaining crew worked the bomb into the lift.

He entered alone, squeezing into the narrow space between the crate and the lift wall.

Lethe had a wide-angled camera view of the top floor. He could see first three men in place. They had more patience than Carlos. They watched the cables rolling through the winches and pulleys as the lift ascended.

The shadow of the truck down by the loading dock had moved away.

Lethe cut the looped video, allowing the live camera feed to reach the front desk again.

The two guards returned to their posts.

"I can hear a lot of scary noises," Carlos said in their ears. The camera image from the lift-feed flickered and for a moment blacked out completely.

When it came back online, the image was shaking violently.

"Carlos?" Morais said.

"This isn't good."

"What's happening?"

"Feels like the cable's going..."

Lethe sent a barrage of fake alarms to the security office masking the genuine ones coming from the lift.

If the cable did fray and fail and the lift plunged... The device wasn't armed. It wasn't going to go off accidentally after a drop like that. Minimal risk, maximum delay, at least for one intended target.

The lift reached the top.

The cable held.

The waiting men helped Carlos manhandle the crate into the corridor. Carlos looked shaken. They moved the bomb to a wide glass double door. Lethe triggered another command at the prompt to spring the lock. The suite was unoccupied. It was as safe a place as they would find to hide the device. It didn't need to stay hidden for long. Just long enough. Again Lethe replaced the rolling feed with a static image in the relay back down to the security office. The office space was huge, modern and mostly open plan. There were floor-to-ceiling windows offering impressive views of the city.

They moved the bomb into place.

"Arm the device," Morais instructed. "We'll do a remote detonator check from here."

Lethe watched Carlos change the pins.

A moment later, Carlos radioed, "We're good to go."

"The detonator's good," Morais confirmed a moment later. "The signal's strong. Post two guards to make sure no one accidentally stumbles on our little surprise. Then get out of there. Good work, Mr Lethe. One more task and you're free to, well, find religion..."

"What's that?"

"Reprogram the door lock for the top floor office."

"Not a good idea. A key card fails, people go and complain, they check it out, chances are someone might notice I've been there. And honestly, the chances are, this place is so antiquated, if you want to change the lock configuration I'll put money you have to be present at the door and use a good old fashioned screwdriver."

If Morais had doubts about what Lethe was telling her, she didn't voice them.

"What I *can* do is stop the elevator from reaching the top."

Morais didn't take her eyes from her screen. She monitored Lethe's every move as he neutralised the problem.

"You really are quite good at this, aren't you, Mr Lethe."

"That's why they pay me the big bucks," he replied.

"Well I'm impressed." She looked at her watch, "The second device should be en route to the feet of Christ the Redeemer. Perhaps this task will test you more. You need to make a helicopter disappear."

"When do we start?"

"You've already started."

TWENTY FIVE

It was weirdly civilised.

Lethe and Cathy were escorted away from Romero's borrowed office to their quarantined dormitory.

They rode the elevator in silence.

Lethe's mind was racing.

There had to be a way to deflect this, to turn the eyes to the chopper somehow, in a way Morais couldn't anticipate.

Something about it bothered Lethe.

When the door closed, he ran it by Cathy. "The Rio bomb."

"What about it? Apart from being unthinkable."

"Romero isn't going to issue a warning," he said. "They're flying the bomb in. There's no way they could hide it at the feet of Christ the Redeemer. Any warning directs the military to exactly where they need to be to neutralise it."

"He's not going to warn Lima either," she said. "And people will refuse to believe Peruvians could possibly inflict this kind of horror on themselves. They'll forget about the internal conflicts and everything else, no eyes will be on the Shining Path and anyone who tries to say the truth will be deemed a conspiracy theorist, like the nutbars who believe 9/11 was an inside job."

"Morais has played us." The weight of the implications hit him hard. He sat down on his bunk with his head in his hands. "We have to stop this," he said. "Whatever it does to us. We're the last resort."

They sat in silence.

The door opened and Morais walked in, as ever flanked by two of her foot soldiers.

"We have to go," the Professor said.

"Rio?" Lethe asked as the guards manhandled him up off the bed.

"Rio can wait. We're moving out."

The sudden haste was curious. First instinct, Noah was free. Or had at least got a message out.

Outside the failing sunlight was bright enough to burn his eyes. The suddenly clear air choked him. A Russian Mi-24P Hind-F helicopter waited near the edge of the plateau, rotors churning up a dust storm. Lethe stumbled as his guards dragged him towards the waiting chopper. They bundled him inside. Cathy was a couple of seconds behind. Morais and the guards jumped in and as she put the helmet on, she spoke to the pilot and he took them up. Airborne, Lethe couldn't hear anything for the deafening engine.

They rose above the dust cloud.

There were more military helicopters rising from the plateau.

In the distance, rounding the peak of a mountain, two very different helicopters approached. Both gunships, almost certainly Russian again. Given the rush Morais's people were in, these two weren't loyal to their cause.

Their wingman was a smaller transport helicopter, a Sikorsky.

The third aircraft struggled to get off the ground.

Lethe watched the two military gunships close in on it, like angry hornets targeting a wounded animal.

And in that moment Lethe knew exactly what that third helicopter was; a decoy.

It had one job, and like suicide bombers willing to die for their cause, it had a single occupant, a pilot willing to die for what he believed in to make sure the others got away. He couldn't imagine commanding such blind loyalty from a man willing to die just so you could live.

He glanced at Morais.

She in turn watched the scene intently. She held her satellite phone but hadn't started dialling.

Two missiles streaked across the sky, burning vapour trails.

They struck the Sikorsky, ripping into it. The helicopter went up in a brief, intense fireball that burned brighter than the Incan sun. The second gunship peeled away in pursuit of the other two target choppers, both were still very much in range.

Morais pressed the button, triggering the Nazi fail-safes built into the facility.

For a heartbeat nothing, silence owned the mountain and then all hell broke loose as the mountain's peak erupted. The explosion was incredible, the world tearing itself in two, the mountain suddenly raining down from the sky. The blast pummelled their bird, battering it sideways and sending it spinning. A huge cloud of rock dust enveloped the plateau. The pilot battled for control, fighting the shockwave, before the helicopter righted itself.

Lethe scrambled to the open doorway.

He started out at the drop.

Half of the mountaintop was gone; utterly obliterated.

The plateau was completely buried.

Huge chunks of rock and debris still fell from the ruined peak.

The metal-lined chambers were nowhere to be seen. The two gunships gone, either caught up in the blast or crushed by raining debris.

A moment later, a second explosion came, resounding deep down in the valley floor.

Lethe grabbed a pair of ear defenders. The roar of the engines reduced to a dull throbbing.

He wasn't a religious man, but he couldn't help but think that but for the grace of God he could have been in any of those other birds. The Mi-24P Hind-F rounded another mountain peak, and moments later the devastation passed out of view.

Cathy reached out and took his hand.

If nothing else, it stopped his hand from shaking.

TWENTY SIX

They flew through the night.

Lethe didn't sleep. Cathy lay curled up on one of the benches along the side wall.

There were twenty of them on board, as well as an extensive rack of weapons and ammunition. The bird was roughly similar in size to a carriage on the London Underground, and had the same ceiling. Tattered padding covered a patch above his head. An old Argentinian flag had been sewn into the fabric. The pervasive odour of diesel underscored the disrepair.

There was a drop ramp out of the back. No one was standing guard. He could, theoretically, jump.

But then what?

He glanced to his left, away from Cathy, at the soldier sleeping beside him. She was snoring gently, her head tipped back at an awkward angle. Lethe noticed something clipped to her belt.

It was a satellite phone.

Making a move for it would get them both thrown off the ramp, but he couldn't stop himself. He wasn't thinking straight. He had been scared for so long the glimpse of a light at the end of it all, a tiny ray of hope, was enough to make him do something stupid. He inched his hand towards the soldier's belt.

Lethe's fingers grazed the phone.

He wasn't a pickpocket and the angle was awkward but he could just get two fingers around it. Slowly, slowly, slowly, he teased it upwards, easing it a couple of millimetres at a time. He didn't dare breathe. The rest of his body was absolutely tense. Beyond tense. Rigid. Another couple of millimetres. A few more. *Come on*, he urged the universe. *Give me a break. Just this once and I won't ask for you for anything again.*

The phone lifted free, but two fingers were never going to be enough to hold it.

It slipped through his digits, falling to the metal floor.

He couldn't snake a hand out; someone would be drawn by the sudden movement, even if they looked like they were sleeping, they almost certainly weren't. Not all of them.

He cushioned the fall with his foot, preventing it from spinning away. The deafening *chop chop chop* of the rotors was more than enough to mask that muffled impact.

Lethe hooked his toe around it and edged the phone very gradually until it rested between his feet.

One of the men opened their eyes, looking straight at him. Lethe shifted in his seat, pretending to go back to sleep.

It wouldn't win him any Oscars, but it was enough to fool the terrorist.

He couldn't risk leaning forward to lift the phone now. It was just going to have to stay there between his feet until he could safely reach down.

If he ever could.

TWENTY SEVEN

The early morning sun burned red on the horizon as they came in to land.

Lethe had spent the last hour looking at the faces of the men and women in the helicopter with him. Directly opposite was a young woman, barely out of her teens, with features carved out of basalt. She was twitchy. She kept clenching and unclenching her left hand, a nervous tick. The man beside was forty years older, granite to her black rock. His beard was more salt than pepper, and his eyes were a piercing blue.

Lethe stretched dramatically, feigning coming to, rubbed his thighs to work the circulation a little, then made a show of reaching down to adjust his boots. He didn't look up as he palmed the phone, slipped it into the cuff of his boot and tucked his trouser over it.

Morais walked the line between her people.

She barked a brusque order in Portuguese. The meaning was clear: *Go go go!* The men and women of the Shining Path followed orders, rising and hefting their weapons and backpacks.

They filed out of the aircraft.

General Romero waited for them on the hardstand.

Lethe blinked in the sunshine. They'd put down on a helipad on the roof of a building. Almost certainly a hospital, given the double doors that led directly to a lift, but he didn't see any of the familiar icons of medicine, no red cross, no caudacus. Just more Spanish.

There were no immediately obvious landmarks, which meant not Rio, Lima. He didn't recognise anything from a week ago. Was it really that recent?

Behind them, the helicopter lifted into the air. It was an impressive sight, not that Lethe got to enjoy it as one of the terrorists grabbed him by the scruff of the beck and propelled him towards the stairwell, then pushed, so he stumbled the first six or seven steps. He barely caught his balance, grabbing at the handrail to stop himself from falling a lot further. They descended the ten flights to the ground, no conversation, only the deafening echo of their feet on the concrete steps, until they stepped out into the outside world.

Two battered minibuses were parked up kerbside. Lethe saw medical waste containers and recycling bins side by side.

Half of Morais's crew piled in to one vehicle, half into the other.

"The second device should be entering Brazilian air space soon. Time for you to earn your keep, Mister Lethe. Make sure it arrives safe and sound."

Lethe said nothing.

It was good to be in Lima.

Noah was here, somewhere. It was about time for a big mushy reunion with that reckless bastard again. All he needed were a couple of seconds with the phone to give him a signal to trace. He didn't feel helpless anymore.

It took an hour and then some to navigate the crawl of Lima's insane morning traffic.

They turned off the road, driving down a short concrete ramp, and pulled up inside an abandoned customs warehouse in a beaten down part of town. The air tasted of exhaust fumes. More Shining Path were there to meet them. He was beginning to realise the true scope of Romero's operation. They had resources.

The second bus drove into the building behind them.

Lethe caught Morais's eye. "Hey Prof, not to be pain, but I've really got use the bathroom."

"I don't think so."

"You really don't want me to shit myself, Prof. It will turn pretty fucking ugly pretty fucking fast, if you get my meaning."

"Fine. You two," she gestured to two of her men, "Make sure our guests are freshened up." There was a single toilet door in the far corner of the warehouse, beside an enclosed office.

As they walked across the warehouse floor, Cathy whispered, "Don't help them. Not to keep me alive."

"What?" said Lethe.

"My life for millions. I'm ready to die. I've made my peace with it, Jude."

"I'm not going to let you die."

"Yes you are. And do you know why? Because I'm leverage. That's the only reason I'm still alive. They threaten me, you do whatever they want. It needs to stop. I could take myself out of the equation right now," she said, a slightly manic edge to her voice.

"Shut up," one of their two guards said, barely managing those two words in English.

"If I die then you're free. You can stop this."

Cathy was louder now. The guard drove the butt of his gun into her gut, doubling her up. She straightened, slowly, and he could see it in her eyes, that change. She wanted to die. Ronan had talked about it before, seeing it in people's faces when they were looking to commit suicide by cop. It was a terrifying transformation.

Morais was only a few steps behind, heading towards the office with the general.

"Calm yourself, girl," the general said, not unkindly. He almost looked like he felt sorry for her, which somehow made what they were doing to her worse, not better.

Cathy shook her head. "I'm done. I'm through. I'm getting off the ride," Cathy said.

"Stop it," Lethe told her, but Cathy wasn't listening.

"You want to die?" Morais drew her pistol and slid the barrel action, chambering a round. She aimed it at Cathy's head.

"Yes. I *want* you to shoot me. I want you to –"

Morais pistol whipped her across the temple with the butt of the gun. As Cathy dropped to her knees, she said "You can't always get what you want. Now use the toilet or don't use the toilet, I don't care."

The Professor turned and followed Romero into the office, slamming the door behind her.

It could have gone better. Lethe opened the toilet door, stepping aside to let her use it first.

The sound of running made him turn. He saw the woman from the helicopter—whose phone was currently tucked inside the cuff of his boot—rushing towards the office.

He turned back to the toilet door, doing his best to appear nonchalant, but his nerves were fraying.

The universe gives and the universe takes away, he thought. *Because everyone knows that the universe is a bastard.*

Cathy opened the bathroom door. At the same moment Morais and the female soldier stepped out of the office. There was blood on Cathy's forehead and cheek from an angry cut.

Lethe held the door with his left hand, giving her room to step around him, and had one foot over the threshold. All he needed was a few seconds.

"Stop!" Morais yelled.

Lethe froze. He looked back over his shoulder.

Morais had her gun aimed at his back.

"I told you not to do anything stupid, Mister Lethe. Hand it over."

Lethe turned slowly, spreading his arms wide, his face all innocence, like butter wouldn't melt. "Sorry?"

"The phone."

"What phone?"

Morais fired a single round. The bullet splintered the wood of the door frame between his and Cathy's head. The report was deafening in the cavernous space.

"Okay, nice and easy," Lethe said. He reached down and drew up his trouser leg. The phone protruded above the cuff. He handed it over.

"You really are an idiot sometimes," said Morais.

She pulled the trigger again.

This time she didn't miss.

She put a bullet in Cathy's head.

Silence followed the deafening noise.

Lethe held his breath as Cathy collapsed against him, a blood red rose punched through the front of her skull.

He caught her and held her. He couldn't let her fall.

"You *cunt*," he spat. "You didn't have to do that."

"I gave her what she wanted. And I taught you a lesson you won't forget. Don't fuck with me, Lethe," Morais said. "I won't allow you to ruin everything. Now put her down and go take your piss."

Lethe couldn't let go of Cathy. The guards had to pin his arms back and drag her away from him, with Lethe fighting them every inch of the way. It was a fight he couldn't win. And it didn't matter. She was dead. They pushed him towards the bathroom.

"Oh, and Mr Lethe," Morais added. He turned and stared at her with dead eyes. "No bullets for you. You try and screw me, I'll have Larkin skinned alive while you watch. It is a barbaric death. I take no pleasure in it, but Castillo is quite skilled. Are we clear?"

"Abundantly," said Lethe.

He went in and closed the door behind him. There was no lock. He sank to the piss-soaked floor with his back against the door and cried, wretched uncontrollable tears, for everything he'd done wrong. His entire body heaved with the wracking sobs.

Morais banged on the door.

He didn't move.

She banged on the door again.

Still he didn't move.

He wasn't done grieving. Not yet.

But he couldn't stay there on the floor crying. He needed to bottle it for however long it took to put an end to this hell he was living through, and mourn for her later. Eventually he forced himself to his feet. He had no more time for grieving. He knew he had to move quickly. Morais was going down. Her and her tinpot fucking militia. She could bluster and threaten everyone and anything he had ever loved, it didn't matter. They held no weight, because the only people he cared about were his team, and every single one of them would give their life in a heartbeat to stop a bitch like Morais.

Unwittingly, she'd actually given him a shred of good news: Noah was alive.

That meant salvation.

Meantime, he'd do what he had to do. And when the opportunity to fight back arrived, he'd seize it without hesitation. He had nothing to lose.

What he did have was simple.

He had motivation.

TWENTY EIGHT

There was no one with a cardboard sign waiting to meet Ronan Frost as he walked into the arrivals hall at Jorge Chávez International Airport.

He liked it that way.

The Irishman moved through the crowds of people, hearing twelve languages in as many steps, as friends and relatives met, lovers kissed and children ran around excitedly. All of human life was here, he thought, and he had no place being amongst it. He preferred it that way. He had travelled light, only carry-on, so he was through customs before anyone else on his flight.

His suit looked rumpled and slept in, which was exactly what it was, but it was still a three-thousand-pound piece of tailoring.

He headed for the car rental desk.

Habit had him run through a number of defensive measures, using reflections to check behind him for anyone looking to pick up his tail. He was exhausted after the hours in the air and almost as long waiting for connecting flights from Warsaw.

It was 2pm local time. The increased security was obvious, and for most tourists, not comforting. Soldiers packing serious firepower didn't do much for holiday makers, but after the Machu Picchu attacks he'd honestly expected more.

His instructions were vague. Vaguer than the whole Crocea Mors debacle. The old man was distraught. He'd spent most of the call cursing himself for sending Lethe into hell. Noah was here somewhere but hadn't checked in for several days. The job was simple enough, bring their people home. Beyond that, stop her, whoever she was. Konstantin was on his way to Rio; and actually, given the connections might well be in situ already. The old man didn't say why, only that he was acting on intel. They didn't argue. They did what they were told.

Frost had no technical backup.

He was used to the familiar—and incessant—background chatter from Lethe in his ear.

The old man was poor substitute for Jude.

So with no idea where to start, and nobody tapping into satellite feeds to guide him, Frost was going to need to rely on good old fashioned legwork and grey matter to find his people.

The obvious first port of call was Machu Picchu, see if he could pick up a trail. The terrorists had moved out, planning something bigger than massacring a few dozen tourists. The old man had intel to indicate that the bad guys had been searching for something, though whether they had found it or not he didn't know.

He wasn't here to solve the plot.

His instructions were to find Noah and Jude and bring them home.

What worried Frost was just what a terrorist cell could do with a man of Jude Lethe's talents. No computer system in the world was safe from him, and computers governed everything these days. He was, and Frost had said it any number of times, the most dangerous member of the team because he had the skills to bring the world to its knees in a series of shock events designed to cause maximum chaos. And the old man knew that, too. Why the hell he'd sent him to this godforsaken place and then allowed Noah to leave him alone defied reason.

The line at the rental desk wasn't moving.

Frost had never been the most patient soul.

He broke from the line and headed for the taxi rank, intending to buy a driver for the day.

The queue here was considerably longer, but moving fast, with ushers pointing people hurriedly left and right into cabs as they pulled up to the kerb.

He watched a very shaky video of the Machu Picchu attack on the small screen of his phone. It was his tenth time of viewing the worst of it. That the footage had made it this far was a miracle, but given the universe was playing fast and loose with the rules he'd have traded it for a bigger miracle with better footage. The camera work wasn't great in that the camera roved so wildly it there was almost no focus when it came to faces. Lethe would have been able to do something with it, somehow, but he wasn't Lethe. Ronan had Google. The accounts he'd found from survivors varied wildly, as though they'd gone through entirely different experiences, which was often the case with traumatic events. The only thing the majority agreed upon was that the terrorists both looked and sounded South American. That narrowed down the options. The most obvious was the Shining Path, or it would have been if it wasn't a relic of the past. It could have been the work of a local terror cell, either working alone or affiliated with a more familiar organization, either home grown or imported.

Frost reached the front of the line. He climbed into the back of a battered old Lincoln Town Car. The smart move was to regroup, settle into a hotel to establish a base of operation, familiarise himself with the territory and then begin whittling down the options. Even cities as large and sprawling as Lima only had so many viable areas for a group with their specific needs. The old man had booked him into one of the upper floors of the Westin. High up inside one of the tallest buildings in Lima, it offered an excellent panoramic view of the city, which he matched up against the cheap tourist map to get his bearings.

TWENTY NINE

The problem with having a reputation was that it brought expectations, which killed the element of surprise.

They moved him out of the cell again.

Time had lost all meaning. He had no idea how long he'd been in there. A couple of days? A week? It was maybe a day, day and a half, since he'd last spoken with the old man and here they were dragging him out to read their dumb scripts again.

If Sir Charles had caught Noah's earlier message, Frost should be in Lima by now.

It was a big if, but he was going to function as if it wasn't.

He looked at his captors.

He'd changed the way he thought about them. Now they were the walking dead.

Right now, though, the bastards were being careful. He was never alone with just one of them, never close enough to make a play for a gun.

The chains had done their work. He couldn't feel his arms; his shoulders were swollen and his back hurt *badly*. Walking was tough. He could barely move. Without his hands he couldn't hold the glass, which meant Carlos had to pour water into his mouth. It dribbled down his chin, soaking his shirt. Food was harder, it hurt to swallow. He brought it up again seconds later. Vomiting was agony beyond anything they'd inflicted on him.

Frost had better hurry or there'd be nothing left of him worth saving.

The problem was, of course, Frost had no idea where he was. He'd not been able to work Barrios Altos into the mayday, and that was even assuming this basement was beneath La Quinta Heeren, but realistically it could have been anywhere. He'd been out of it for the duration. They could have done anything to him in that time.

Carlos's phone rang. He took the call. Noah heard his name mentioned, and a few seconds later, Lethe's. He took it as a sign the kid was alive. There was a newspaper on the table in front of him. If the date was right, it was his fifth day of incarceration.

"Él está aquí," Carlos said, glancing at Noah. "Si. Si. Lo vamos a mantener vivo."

If he remembered right, 'Vivo' meant 'living', and he was fairly sure 'mantener' was *to maintain*. So, through the fog of his pain, he was reasonably sure they were keeping him alive. Maybe as to ensure Lethe played along with whatever they wanted from him. And If he was wrong, he was dead anyway.

Carlos hung up.

"So, Señor Larkin, that time again. Are you ready to phone home?"

"Can't wait."

Carlos made the call. The old man came online within seconds. He'd been waiting for this.

"Noah?"

"Yeah it's me."

"What are you up to?"

"Me? I'm about to spring the three American scientists, you know how it is..."

"Where?"

"La Quinta Heeren," Noah said. It was a calculated gamble. "I got this."

Carlos killed the connection.

"You stupid fuck. You stupid, stupid fuck."

"What?" Noah replied, a sly smile stirring. "It's the only place in Lima I know. What was I supposed to say?"

"Don't play games. You aren't clever. You deliberately gave him our location."

"And told him not to come."

Carlos considered that for a moment, then shook his head. "I don't trust you."

"Big whoop. I don't trust you either. Thing is, you killed the connection. That means you fucked up, buddy boy. The old man's one smart son of a bitch. And thanks to you knows something's up. Twenty-four hours, you'll be in a body bag."

Carlos laughed. "In twenty-four hours everyone in Lima will be in a body bag. Let your people come, they die as well. Now, to hurt you for your smart mouth."

"Hit me with your best shot," Noah said.

He gritted his teeth.

His two guards stepped forward. They made a show of rolling their sleeves up and cracking their knuckles. He wasn't easily intimated, and nothing about these goons worried him. "You can't hurt me," he said. "Because I don't give a shit."

"Maybe we can help you care," the first said as he slammed a fist into Noah's teeth.

Noah spat blood and shook his head.

Another punch, another angle, more blood.

And then they started getting creative, two blows at once, both sides of the head.

Arms chained, there was nothing he could do to stop them. And he was reasonably sure they wouldn't beat him to death.

"Bring it on," he said, lips badly torn up by the flurry of punches that rained down. "I've had better." The pain was welcome. You needed to be alive to hurt. Pain was good. He pushed back against the next blow, and the momentum took his chair over, leaving him on the floor, on his back helpless. The first man stepped in and kicked him brutally in the gut. He felt something give. He lay there. He made no move to struggle or try and wriggle away from the next crippling kick. The guard took a step back, then came in like a footballer looking to put his skull into the back of an invisible net. "Enough," Carlos held up his hand, a fraction of a second before the man landed the devastating blow. He pulled out of the punishing kick, and looked down at Noah. "Next time," he said.

"Promises, promises," Noah said, only no one in the room could understand a word he said.

"Put him back in his cell."

Noah didn't resist. He let them drag him back into the dark.

The old man called it a *zugzwang*—they were compelled to move, but in doing so considerably weakened their own position. This was the kind of shit the old man lived for.

Noah almost felt sorry for the bastards, but he was pretty sure they'd broken a couple of his ribs.

THIRTY

Lethe was going through a crisis of faith. His world was digital. His entire existence was the ones and zeroes of the online world, and here, now, right at that very second, he detested everything about the computer in front of him and what it represented.

Yes, he could shut down the power feed into this shithole of a warehouse, he could trigger alerts to the police, and quite possibly electrocute half of Morais's men, but it was all so pointless against what was coming. And after his little stunt with the phone the Professor wasn't taking her eyes off him. Every keystroke. Every mouse click. It was all mirrored back to her screen. Sacrificing himself now might delay the attacks. It might buy Frost, Koni and Orla the time to change the way it played out. It might be enough to make a difference.

But dying for that many *mights* wasn't smart thinking.

A pang of guilt and grief struck Lethe. It rose up from nowhere to become the entirety of his world. Morais watched her screen. Even though there was nothing to look at, she didn't look away. Wrapped up inside that guilt and grief was an overwhelming sense of hopelessness that he couldn't let himself surrender to. So no, when it came time to check out, he was doing it on his terms, when the *mights* turned into *woulds*.

That was his first real glimpse of what kept Noah, Frosty and the others going when normal people would shut down. It was a peek into the mindset of his friends and what motivated them not to fail, even when confronted with the impossible. People like that, broken people, ended up making the world better. That was ironic.

And for now that burned within him.

It scared him.

Morais spoke. "You've added the delivery to the schedule."

Lethe nodded, but because she wasn't looking at him he needed to vocalise his response. It was hard to keep his tone neutral. "I logged damage to Christ's right hand, then placed a work order for the replacement backdated two months. They'll be expecting the shipment to arrive today."

"And security has it on their schedule?"

Lethe clicked on another window and highlighted the delivery on the day's agenda.

"Of course they do."

"Air Traffic Control?"

The sites were all in Portuguese, but the code behind them was all the same, so they presented no more of a challenge than getting into the London Transport network or the Paris Metro. The problem was the machine. It was just too slow for his purposes, millions of calculations a second slower than his own machine. Airspace monitoring systems were protected by layers upon layers of encryption and security. It wasn't like he could just magically open a backdoor, he needed to fake-out a handshake and make the recipient think it knew who it was talking to. That's where the certification came from. And, in that lay Lethe's genius.

It was impossible to spoof the handshake. The levels of encryption involved were the foundation of the internet.

Without the trust that these things worked the whole commercial hub was vulnerable. But Lethe was good at the impossible. He'd rooted the digital handshake authentication and rebuilt the code around it to allow his rig to impersonate anyone and everyone he needed to be.

The Aviation authority's machines welcomed him as one of their own.

He didn't bother explaining how he'd done it, or why he'd needed two programs off his own laptop to do it. He told her, "This is the part in the film where they show the montage of me doing clever stuff, but not the real stuff that I'm doing because that's mind-numbingly boring to watch." She laughed at that, but gave him a level of autonomy to do his thing without constant questions. "The thing I can't do is implant memories in the people working at the monument. Those orders weren't there yesterday."

"You know as well as I do that people trust what their all-knowing computers tell them. They'll convince themselves they missed it. After all, it's always been there."

Thirty minutes later, the job was done.

He hit the last keystroke, knowing he was signing his own death warrant. "So," he said. "I guess this is the part where you kill me."

"No no no, Mister Lethe, don't you understand yet? You are an asset, and your value will only increase in the days after the bombs. You have a gift, as you've proven. I will be looking to you to rebuild the security networks of both countries in our own image, including coordinating the military as they unite under the Shining Path's banner. Why would I kill you when you have the skills we need to provide stability at a time of great unrest and fear? You can help us communicate the new leadership structure to the population. And of course in this era of fake news, you can make sure there is a convincing evidentiary trail to lay the blame for these heinous bombs at the feet of Middle Eastern terrorists. The possibilities are endless when it comes to a man with your resources. And of course, when we are through, I want you to go home too."

She was lying, obviously.

A little knowledge was a deadly thing. He was the only one with the skillset to expose her, and to give lie to the story she'd force him to weave around her actions. And she'd know he was smart enough to know that. So how did he play it?

"You don't need to lie to me," he said eventually. "I know how this is going to go down. I was dead the moment I set foot in this country, I just didn't know it."

"It doesn't have to be that way, Jude," she said, choosing to use his first name for the first time in a long while. He knew she was trying to placate him, connect, foster some sort of Stockholm-Syndrome bond between them. He wasn't buying what she was selling, but she was persistent. "All I am asking of you is that you help us achieve what needs to be done. Help us create a new South America, a unified land, where everyone gets enough to eat, where nobody is vulnerable or exploited by the rich men of the world. It will be a beautiful continent, Jude. And just imagine, you will be an architect of peace. We are the catalyst, the spark, but with your help we will enrich the lives of millions of people. Everything that happens to make that new life possible for my people is a price worth paying. But I am not a fool. I know you haven't come around to our way of thinking yet. I know you don't understand. It is a pity."

General Romero entered the room carrying two mugs of coffee. He set one down in front of Morais and drank from the other. He hadn't brought one for Lethe.

"Milk, two sugars, thanks," Lethe said.

"When you are finished. Making progress?" the general asked.

Morais didn't take her eyes from the screen. "Close. All of the pieces are in play."

"And is Mister Lethe behaving himself?"

"He is an angel," Morais said. "Now. He just needed to be brought to heel."

"Most excellent. We do, however, have one problem. It would appear that we are compromised. Larkin gave away the location of the safe house."

"Doesn't matter," Morais reasoned. "No way they can get forces here in time to prevent the detonation."

"Carlos has been instructed to put down Larkin and the hostages. They are no longer worth the trouble of keeping them alive."

"Would Wyndham reach out to local law enforcement?"

"No, he knows we have people in place."

"Very good. Keep me informed."

"Of course."

Romero left the room. Morais frowned at her screen.

"Shouldn't you be working?"

Lethe had been listening intently to the conversation. He returned to his work. "Waiting for my coffee,"

"For pity's sake, here, take mine," Morais slid her mug across the table towards him.

Lethe reached out for it, and as he did so, made a deliberately clumsy move, knocking the steaming mug over. Boiling hot liquid splashed over Morais's hand.

She flinched, pulling back, her chair dragging across the floor as she stood. She cursed, clamping her hand between her legs.

"You need to get cold water on that," Lethe said, as the two guards instinctively stepped towards her to help.

"Not me, you idiots, him." she yelled, waving her good hand at Lethe.

Lethe had finished typing and hit send as the butt of a rifle cracked into the side of his head. He pitched sideways out of the chair and sprawled across the floor, clutching at his face.

He expected a second blow that never came.

Morais stood over his computer, cradling her burned hand but ignoring the pain.

"Oh, Mr Lethe," *no longer on first name terms*, Lethe thought. *That didn't last long.* "That was *really* stupid."

Romero came into the room, drawn by the sudden commotion. More guards flanked him.

"What the hell is going on?"

"This idiot just emailed the *Ministerio de Defensa* from our encoded account. "

"They'll know it's Shining Path behind the attack," Lethe said from the floor. "You can't pretend anymore."

"What did it say?"

"Two words: 'Bomb Lima'."

"*Mierda.*"

Morais's expression was cold fury. And then her face softened and she started to smile. "No. We can use this. They will be looking for a bomb," she looked down at Lethe. "So let's give them one."

THIRTY ONE

"Just go. Run. Leave me," Flynn cried. Tears of defeat tracked down her face. "Go!"

She tried to shove Lethe away from her, but he wasn't going anywhere.

"No, we go out together," he said. His gaze darted between the bomb vest Flynn wore and the TV News camera crew filming them, and then from those vultures to the circle of armed police officers. The officers approached slowly, walking up the cathedral steps one at a time.

"You don't even know me."

"I don't need to."

"Well, I know who you are," Flynn said.

"My fame precedes me."

"Morais never needed me. That's the truth. They kidnapped me and my friends to get you here. That means my vest is the live one. They don't want to hurt you when they still need you."

Everything she said made sense. Of course he was more valuable, in terms of Morais's game plan at least.

Unless this was a double-bluff and he was *expected* to think his was the dummy vest. He would try to save Flynn because that was who he wanted to be, the hero Cathy had deserved and he had failed to become.

Maybe both vests were live. All they needed was one to blow, and that gave the authorities the bomb Lethe had warned them about—right here in one of the busiest spots in all of Lima. She'd made her point. Not for the first time Lethe wished he'd had another second to add the word "nuclear" to his message.

Morais's voice spoke in his ear. "I thought you might like to know that Christ the Redeemer is live. You've been a wonderful distraction. Everyone's been watching you instead of the bomb. It's all very exciting. Will the police stop the terrorists at *Plaza de Armas*? Will the bomb go off? It's reality television at its finest. All we've got to do is give them a bloody end."

"Fuck you!" Lethe said. He had no idea if Morais could hear him, but it didn't matter. He'd not said it for her benefit.

Flynn blinked and took a step backwards, mistaking the direction of his anger. Her sudden movement sent ripples through the cops, but by some miracle, no one opened fire.

Lethe barked out an equally harsh laugh, and shook his head, "No, not you." Lethe tapped his ear with his free hand. "Morais is in my head."

It took Flynn a moment, then she asked, "She's talking to you?"

And then Lethe knew for certain. Morais's conversation was for his ears only. This was a test for him. Apart from the vest and the bomb, Flynn was utterly irrelevant. She was a distraction meant to keep him guessing. But, by putting the decision of who should die in Lethe's hands she'd confirmed Flynn's vest was the live one.

The cops were ten feet away. They were trying to cut the angles off, working themselves around so that they stood between the pair and the cathedral doors.

Lethe ignored them.

Sticks of C4 padded out Flynn's vest. Without going over it thoroughly, the workmanship looked decent. It wasn't homebrew. There were no obvious loose wires to tug on, and release straps on the vest would trigger the detonator. He whipped a finger around, telling Flynn to turn. She spun around without question. He examined the plastic snaps at the back. They were both interwoven with a length of cable. There was no easy way to tell if they were decorative or live.

But that wasn't his primary concern. His biggest worry was the dead man's switches they each held. Assuming he was right, and his wasn't live, he could let go of his switch.

Unless Morais was a bastard and had his switch primed to trigger Flynn's vest.

Cars streamed into the plaza, among them a second news van. It drew up along the far side of the *Plaza de Armas*. The crew spilled out of the vehicle and raced across the wide square.

It wasn't until he saw the cameraman drop to one knee and focus in presumably on his face that Lethe realised he was fucked.

Morais had set this up.

She'd known the film crews would come.

Which meant she didn't care if the world and his wife saw him.

The nearest cop was just two steps below him now. He held out a hand, motioning to Lethe to pass him the dead man's switch. There was pity in the man's eyes. Did he understand that they were the victims here?

"Give him your switch," Lethe said.

Flynn shook her head. "No. She's watching. If we cross her she'll kill us."

"Stand by me. I think you're right. Stand close to me and she won't kill us. Give him the switch and let the police get the vests off us. They're our way out of this."

Flynn shook her head, but took a step towards the officer with her hand outstretched.

"I don't think so, Mister Lethe," came Morais's voice in Lethe's ear. "If that cop's hand gets within six inches of the switch I'm blowing you all to Kingdom Come."

"Don't," Lethe cried, and this time he meant both of them, and was grateful when Flynn pulled her hand back.

The two camera crews captured the move on camera.

"Time to make peace with your God, Mr Lethe."

"We need more time!"

Flynn didn't. She lashed out, shoving Lethe hard. The unexpected ferocity of the move caught him off balance, and Lethe stumbled. His foot twisted on the edge of the top step, and unbalanced he fell into the officer, and like ungainly dominoes the two went sprawling down the steps.

Above them, Flynn let go of the switch.

THIRTY TWO

Noah was in bad shape.

They dragged him upstairs. There was panic in the complex. He'd done his job. They were running. Some of it was excitement, too. They were agitated.

A TV set on the upper level showed a scene playing out on the steps of the cathedral at *Plaza de Armas* in central Lima. A man and a woman, surrounded by police. He didn't get a good look at their faces but he recognised the bomb vests they wore.

Quietly, he allowed his anger to grow.

The men around him were sloppy. Distracted.

It was all he needed.

As his captor shifted his grip, Noah launched himself.

He went at them like a wild animal.

With a roar, he propelled himself towards the man on the right. He barrelled the man into a wall so hard the plaster shattered. It made no difference that Noah's arms were chained, he couldn't use them anyway. He used what he had: brute force and overwhelming rage. He charged at the second guard, rising up at the last to drive his forehead into the man's face. The impact was sickening. It was greeted by blood and gristle and the man went down puking as he collapsed to the mosaicked tiles on the floor. Reeling, Noah kicked out at the first man, hammering his booted foot up between his legs hard enough so the guy would be tasting his own testicles for a week. With the first man out of the game, Noah set about finishing off the man on the floor, straddling him. He used the chains around his wrist, wrapping them around the fallen man's neck, and with a savage jerk started to choke the life out of him. The chains bit deep, cutting into the guard's throat. There was blood, and a few seconds later there was piss as the man clawed at the chain, kicking out desperately as Noah choked the life out of him.

It felt fucking marvellous to hurt someone finally.

He heard a shot. Nothing hit him so he didn't worry about it. And another, then another in quick succession. Seven in total.

The man died between his legs. He carried on choking him until he felt a hand clasp his shoulder.

He lashed out, snarling—only to be greeted by Ronan Frost's wry smile.

"I can't believe you needed me to come in and save your ugly arse, mate, that's got to be a sickener," Frost said.

"I had it under control," Noah told him.

"I can see that."

Noah turned back towards the TV. Six dead bodies lay in front of it, bullet wounds leaking blood over the floor.

"I left you one," Frost said, reloading his Browning.

Noah saw Carlos, slumped up against a wall. He clutched at his gut. Blood oozed through his fingers from a hole that Frost had made.

Noah nodded. "That was actually very decent of you, Frosty."

"Don't take it personally. First one didn't put him down. Didn't have a second because I ran out of bullets." Frost shrugged.

He walked over to Carlos and took a set of keys from his top pocket. Then returned to Noah and released his arms.

Noah dropped to his knees. His arms hung uselessly at his sides. "You want this?" Frost offered him a gun, but he couldn't take it. He shook his head. Instead, he forced himself back up to his feet and lurched towards Carlos. He dropped down again, this time just inches from the terrorist's face.

"You know, in a different place, different time, you and me… nah, who am I trying to kid? You're a dick, Carlos. I would call you a cunt, but that's just demeaning to my favourite part of the female anatomy and I don't want to be thinking about you the next time I see one. So, we'll leave it at dick. This doesn't end well for you."

Carlos let out a groan as another wave of black agony washed over him.

"Don't try and move," Noah said as more blood pumped from the terrorist's stomach wound. "Not if you want to live."

A trickle of blood escaped the corner of Carlos's mouth.

"Where were you taking me?"

Carlos coughed, crying out as the movement brought fresh pain and more blood loss.

"A warehouse on Jirón Lucanas at Rivas, La Victoria district."

Noah turned to Frost. "You know where that is?"

"Not a clue," Frost replied. "But I know a man who does."

"My gun?" Noah asked Carlos.

"Lock box, by the door on the way in. There's a shelf." Carlos tipped his head back and moaned in pain.

Noah stood shakily. Frost tried to help him, but Noah shook his head. Frost got the message and turned his attention to the TV.

"The bad news is you don't survive. Mostly because I don't want you to."

"Please," Carlos said, his head lolling and his hands trying uselessly to plug the leak in his guts.

"Don't beg. It's unbecoming," Noah said. "Now, listen to this because this is the serious part. I want you to take this to the grave with you," he punctuated his words with a kick squarely in Carlos's face. "I." *Kick.* "Fucking." *Kick.* "Hate." *Kick.* "The." *Kick.* "Shining." Carlos's face was a bubbling mass of blood, snot and shattered bone. Noah couldn't tell if he was alive or dead. He decided to be sure. He drew back his leg and delivered a final shattering blow that crunched through the man's skull.

Carlos slumped to the floor.

"I didn't think it was a bad book," Frost said. "Not one of King's best. Or do you mean the movie?"

"Path," Noah finished.

"Holy shit," said Frost. "What the fuck is Jude doing on TV?"

Noah's attention snapped to the screen.

He saw Lethe standing at the top of the cathedral steps, one of the two people wearing the suicide vests.

"Crap. What's the idiot got himself into now?" Noah growled.

The woman with Lethe shoved him *hard* and as he fell let go of something. A dead man's switch?

The explosion was huge. The shockwave hurled the cameraman backwards, and in the seconds that followed the detonation the screen showed only sky, quickly obscured by smoke and dust.

Frost and Noah rushed for the entrance.

"There are other prisoners here," Noah said.

"I'm not here for them," Frost said, looking frantically for the lockbox. It was where Carlos had promised. He lifted the box and smashed it repeatedly against the wall until the lock sprang. Frost took the Heckler and Koch USP 9mm from the box and stuffed it into Noah's empty holster.

"Time to go bring our boy home."

THIRTY THREE

In that second Lethe didn't know if he was alive or dead or trapped somewhere in between.

He didn't believe in an afterlife, so that limited his options.

His eyes were clogged shut with dust and dirt. He could barely breathe; his mouth and nose were choked full of debris. A tinnitus chorus filled his ears, banging on the drums like he'd swallowed a smoke alarm. He couldn't hear any real sounds. Only the noises of his own body from the inside. He gagged and coughed and felt his lungs convulsing, rebelling against the shit clogging them up. Incredible pressure bore down on his spine. Crushing him.

Blindly, Lethe pushed out.

Something rolled off. Something limp. The weight relieved some of the pain on his body, but he was still pinned beneath all manner of rubble. He was on his stomach, the concrete steps digging into his gut. He pushed against the ground, trying to squirm free from beneath the debris and crawl down the rubble strewn concrete steps.

His hand came down on something distressingly *wet*.

He coughed again, desperate to clear his lungs.

He felt as though he was drowning.

The rock dust scraped against his face and hands and he still couldn't' open his eyes.

Then abject terror struck him; what if they were gone? What if this was his world now, darkness and thundering aftershocks drumming inside his skull demanding to be let out?

Finally, he felt one eye open. Even so, he couldn't see through thick choking cloud of dust. The fog of debris settled slowly, clearing enough for him to make out shapes moving in front of his face. No details, just amorphous black forms. And then he felt his guts twist and dry heaved a mouthful of acid and bile.

People screamed and car alarms blared, but he could hear none of it for the cacophony that had taken up residence inside his head.

He put a hand to his temple.

There was blood on his hand when he took it away.

Someone grabbed him. He didn't fight it. They dragged him away from the blast zone. Someone had a hand on his vest strap at the shoulder. He realised he'd lost his dead man's switch in aftermath of the explosion.

He tried to speak, but nothing came out.

He desperately tried to protest his innocence, but all he could do was cough and wheeze as they hauled him down the steps and out of the shadow of the cathedral.

A fresh wave of guilt tore through Lethe. He'd failed another woman who needed him.

No.

She'd made a choice. It hadn't been about him saving her. She had saved him. She'd sacrificed herself.

More arms picked him up.

They carried him across the plaza towards the bank of police vans and ambulances. Double doors opened, then he felt himself being bundled inside—as the doors slammed closed, shutting out the chaos—he realised it was a police van, not an ambulance. The muffling of the cacophony outside of his body only intensified the ringing in his ears. He tried to speak, but his voice sounded utterly alien. He wasn't alone in the van. There was someone on a bench seat at the back. Blinking through the tears he realised they were in civilian garb. He struggled to focus.

Morais.

Her fake officers pinned him down.

The van started up. He felt it pull away. In seconds it was moving fast, sirens blaring. The vibration of the engine jarred Lethe's spine.

"Well, wasn't that *fun?*" Morais asked. They were the first words he'd been able to hear in several minutes. He'd have willingly never heard another word if it was a case of trading silence for Morais's life.

One of her men poured water onto his face. Far from being invigorating, the freezing cold had him spitting and lashing out as he struggled to breathe. They held him down again, pouring water over his head. He felt it in his throat, drowning him. He kicked and writhed beneath their pinning hands, bucking against them as they kept on going.

"Calm down," Morais said dispassionately.

But he couldn't.

He couldn't breathe. He was choking on the water and air at the same time, struggling with great gulps, not managing to exhale.

Someone slapped a stinging blow across his face, trying to snap him out of the hysteria.

More water, this time a dribble not a deluge. He tried to drink it down, but it felt like it was flooding his lungs.

When they finally stopped, they hauled him up into a sitting position and left him slumped against the van's wall.

"You didn't have to kill her."

"I didn't. She killed herself. That was her choice."

"I blame," Lethe began, but even those two words were enough to render him breathless. A coughing fit overtook him. "You," he finally managed. There was nothing eloquent about it. He'd wanted to say *for putting that fucking vest on her*, but those seven extra words proved too much.

"The question is, did you learn your lesson? Or do you need more people to die before you do as you are told?"

"I won't... stop... *fighting*."

"Really? Even if Noah Larkin is the next to die? Or how about your precious Charles?"

Lethe said nothing. He needed to preserve what little strength he could muster.

"He's not as safe as he likes to pretend in that dusty old manor house of his."

What she didn't get is when it came down to simple mathematics both Noah and the old man would sacrifice themselves without hesitation if it stopped hundreds of thousands of people dying in their place. And Lethe had learned something important about himself in the last week. He would do the same.

"It won't change anything."

"I know you, Jude, better than you know yourself. When the bombs have gone off you'll do everything you can to help us save lives in the aftermath."

She was right, he realised.

If the bombs did go off, Lethe would work tirelessly to re-establish some form of order to the two devastated countries. That wasn't about helping Morais. That was about humanity.

Relief aid had to get through. Medical assistance needed to be deployed. It would be a nightmare, but he wouldn't stop working to limit the number of people who died in the days that followed of disease, radiation poisoning, violence and unrest, power outages. They would need someone like him trying to stitch the pieces back together into something that could keep the survivors safe.

He shook his head. He wasn't going to let her think she'd won, but they both knew she had.

As the stolen police van reached the warehouse and dipped down the ramp to pass through the entrance, Lethe made himself a promise: there would be no South American "caliphate".

Morais and Romero would hang.

Lethe would make sure of it.

THIRTY FOUR

Frost's driver couldn't get anywhere near the Plaza.

The heavy police and military presence blocked every street leading to Lima's main square, and most of them for about quarter of a mile around, snarling up the traffic even worse than usual.

"Up for a run?" Frost asked.

"No point," Noah said. "Even assuming Jude survived, he's not there now. He'll be on his way to hospital—and as far away from the blast zone as possible. And if he isn't, then the nutty Professor's people grabbed him, and he's gone anyway. So we find her. Driver?"

The man glanced back at Noah through the rear view mirror. "Please, Señor, my name is Martin."

"Do you know La Victoria?"

"Si, of course."

"Fantastic. Next stop Jirón Lucanas and Rivas."

Martin didn't reply.

Instead, he slammed the taxi into reverse, ignoring the other traffic on the road, and nearly rammed into the radiator grille of the car behind, earning them the fury of horns and gesticulations through the open windows. He shifted the gear stick into first with a crunch, missing the clutch, and hit the accelerator with such force the car mounted the pavement in a burn of rubber. And they were away, pedestrians cursing them as they leapt out of their path. Martin wove through the bumper to bonnet traffic, finding gaps and making others where there were none.

He mounted the kerb again, cutting a corner, then he squeezed in between market stalls, racing down a narrow side street that was off-limits for cars. Red lights and traffic laws meant nothing. He raced through Lima.

"I like this guy," said Noah, "He drives like my mum." He sat in the back seat, trying to keep himself upright as Martin threw the car around a ridiculously tight turn. "Where did you find him?"

"You don't find Martin, Martin finds you," Frost said.

Martin responded by slamming on the brakes six inches from smashing into the high steel bumper of an open-backed truck laden with fruit. He ripped off a stream of Spanish invective and reversed just far enough to negotiate the slow moving truck and hurtle on through the streets again.

Kids played a game of football on the cobbles up ahead, using plastic bags for shirts to separate the teams. Martin leaned on his horn, causing them to scatter as he drove through the middle of their makeshift pitch.

The feeling was slowly returning to Noah's extremities. His muscles still burned, and would be agony for days.

In the front, Frost talked with one finger in his ear.

"Yeah, I'm with Noah. You saw Lethe? Not good. We're going after Morais now. Yes sir. Yes, we will. We can't be sure. Yes, we'll bring him home, you have my word. Understood, sir. Yes, I'm well aware we'll be going in blind. We'll be... *careful*. Noah?" Frost glanced back at him. "He looks like shit, but you know Noah, that's pretty much par for the course." A nod, a beat of silence, and then he said, "Frost out."

"Jude's going to have a shit fit when he realises the old man's been playing with his toys."

"We're here," Martin announced.

"Brilliant," Frost said.

"You're a legend, Marty, an absolute ledge," Noah said.

"But this is where I leave you. Sorry. There are places we don't go. This is one."

"That's okay, Martin. We've got it from here."

Frost got out and opened the back door so Noah could tumble awkwardly onto the pavement.

"Mate, you really aren't very graceful, are you?"

"Primo ballerina."

Frost didn't correct him.

The taxi didn't hang about.

Frost pulled his Browning and checked the ammunition. Noah gritted his teeth and reached for his own weapon. He had trouble gripping it, but after a moment nodded, gun pointed at the ground. "Let's do this thing."

Tensing his hands to prevent the gun from slipping through his fingers took every ounce of willpower he had, and his arms *ached* like a bitch. But again, the pain was *good*. It meant that his arms were coming back to life.

"You can stay here if you like," Frost said.

"Have you met me?" Noah replied.

Frost smiled.

The building was a three-storey brick construction sandwiched between two taller office blocks. The whole building was reminiscent of a child's attempt to build houses out of Lego. There was a mixture of different coloured bricks used in the construction of each, and little to suggest any attention had been paid to structural integrity. The whole lot looked like it might collapse in a strong wind.

The warehouse's drab exterior included a balcony on the second floor. Iron bars were in place to prevent anyone from falling, or from getting in. The brickwork was uneven, with large chunks crumbling away. There wasn't a single straight line in sight. On the ground floor he eyeballed a large faded-green loading door. Nearer to them was a second point of entry, this one a similarly weathered door entrance.

No windows on the lower level.

He scanned his surroundings. A good operative gleaned as much as he could about the territory before he made his move. It was all about limiting exposure. There was an auto repair shop opposite, surrounded by more featureless walls and colourful buildings. What he didn't see was anything else that could even vaguely fit the description of a warehouse. So this must be the place.

"Big fan of going in the front door," Frost said with a grin.

"We can even knock first, if you want to make sure it's a fair fight."

THIRTY FIVE

Lethe sat on the floor with his back to the wall.

His head throbbed like a bastard had taken a baseball bat to it.

His throat burned raw.

But he could see.

All things considered, that was a bonus.

His body hurt in places he didn't know could hurt. His clothes were blackened, scorched and pocked with small burn holes. There were patches of someone else's shirt fused to his own. The colour was a match for Lima's police uniforms. The memory came flooding back; him tumbling down the steps with the man still reaching out a hand for the dead man's switch, beneath him. The explosion, and then the awareness of something heavy pinning him. The cop had saved his life by taking the brunt of the explosive force, acting as a human shield.

His body count was multiplying aggressively.

Lethe shuddered.

Morais's people were in the process of moving out. They worked in teams loading supplies, explosives and weapons into the police van, while the last man poured petrol into the tank of a battered 90s Subaru Impreza.

Morais and Romero emerged from the office, still deep in conversation. The Professor carried a gun and her cell phone. She'd transmit the signal over the network to the detonators installed in both bombs, and it would be goodnight Lima, adios Rio. They were inside the blast radius, so if she hit the button now, it'd be crispy fried Lethe, too. Because of the height of the explosion, the devastation wouldn't be as widespread as the bomb over Hiroshima, but it would vaporise everything within a couple of miles and in the immediate vacuum that followed, the air pressure shockwave would flatten every building in its path for another five miles in every direction.

The radioactive fallout would come later, and a lot of the sickness and damage it wrought would depend on which way the wind blew.

By then, Morais would be far from here.

Seven miles. It wasn't far. Ten to be on the safe side, and to avoid the crush of survivors fleeing the blast.

Romero addressed the people in the room. They looked at him with the rapt fascination of disciples watching their messiah on the mount. "In the hours that follow I want you to remember one thing, my friends: our cause is *just*. We are the catalyst for a new world. We are strong enough to make the sacrifice that starts a revolution. Peru will be reborn stronger than ever before. Our brothers and sisters in Brazil will join with us first in grief and then in arms, and we shall see the rise of the most powerful country on the continent. One by one, we will stand with the peoples of every nation in South America, helping the South American Spring. The nations will rise up to overthrow their governments and join our new United Latin American Republic. The ULAR will be born from the ashes and flame of the old world. And it will be glorious."

An enthusiastic cheer went up, masking the sound of the outside door opening.

Two men slipped into the building unnoticed by all but Lethe.

And in that moment his spirits *soared.*

He needed to make himself scarce before the killing began.

He pushed himself to his feet and dived behind a pile of crates, hitting the hardstand as the first shots tore through the warehouse.

Two terrorists were down with head wounds before he was up on his knees. The rest were caught in a moment of indecision, trapped between scattering and fighting back. They couldn't see where the shots had come from. Then the first volley was returned, bullets cutting through the steel door to leave a ragged line of fading sunlight in their wake, and they snapped out of it. Their first instinct was to find cover, some behind the van, others behind the stacks of crates and piles of wood that cluttered the warehouse floor.

Ronan Frost and Noah Larkin came in hot.

They wove a deadly path quickly back and forth across the warehouse, laying down covering fire. It was a shock and awe attack. But in the dust-filtered light it was obvious Noah wasn't moving freely. He looked a mess and was struggling to raise his arm high enough to shoot. Even so, shoot he did, taking out one of the Shining Path's women who was naive enough to put her head up over the line of cover. He didn't miss shots like that.

Frost moved fast, keeping low. He ran across the killing ground, firing with ruthless efficiency; he didn't slow. He ducked and rolled, coming up firing six rounds into two different terrorists, each bullet jerking them around like puppets with their strings cut one at a time. Their machine guns unloaded into the ceiling as they fell, autonomic reflexes squeezing down on the trigger even after they were dead. Frost spun away, hitting the barrier of crates, and rolled with the impact, coming around the corner and up into the face of a man who couldn't pull back in time. Frost shot him twice, once in the gut, once in the heart, and moved on.

A bulky figure stepped out from behind the van, rifle clutched at the ready, but he'd made a mistake, fatally underestimating how much ground Frost had covered.

The Irishman grabbed the barrel of the rifle and drove it *hard* into his stomach.

The terrorist doubled over.

Still holding the barrel, Frost shot him in the face, then pulled him in to use as a human shield as two more of Morais's men charged him. The pair let rip with short bursts of covering fire to buy Morais's and Romero's escape.

Lethe saw the pair scramble into the Impreza. Before he could do anything to stop them, Romero started the engine. The roar and the squealing tires echoed around the space. The Subaru powered towards the darkness at the rear of the warehouse. The loading bay offered them a way out.

Noah emptied his weapon into the rear window, but the Impreza didn't slow even as the glass blew out.

And then it was gone.

A stray bullet slammed into the crate inches from Lethe's face. He pulled back in alarm, and even then it was barely fast enough as the wood splintered again, shredded by another round.

Frost moved to the left, where metal scaffolding had been set up to wash the windows of offices on the upper tier; he jumped, making a grab for the metal bar and used it to lift himself onto the wooden platform. Shots pitted the wall behind him as he launched himself, twisting in mid-air to pull the trigger twice. The first took out the nearest man. It wasn't a clean through and through. It took him in the shoulder and twisted him. Frost hit the ground and rolled, rising to fire again, putting two shots into the second man's centre of gravity. He put another shot into the first man, cleaning up his mess. He stayed low, rolling beneath the chassis of the van.

He reloaded, rising up out of sight now.

Two more shots rang out in rapid succession, their reports echoing around the huge space of the warehouse.

Noah.

A woman on Lethe's side of the van went down clutching her stomach. Another three shots rang out. Two missed. The third turned her face into a bloody mess as she looked towards her murderer.

Lethe couldn't see Frost but he could hear him.

What he did see was a man trying to put a bullet into Frost, but Noah beat him to the punch, his shot taking the man in the shoulder. It was enough to make sure the guy's shot went wide and gave Noah the chance to finish him. Again, it wasn't clean. Two shots this time, one in the chest, one in the neck.

The man died noisily.

Noah looked pissed with himself. A flicker of movement to his left caught his eye. Without thinking he turned, raised his arm and shot—and this time the shot was good. The man didn't stand a chance. Noah roared in pain and clutched his gun arm. Had he been hit? Lethe didn't think so. More of the same injury he'd arrived with. What had Morais's people done to him?

Frost emerged from hiding, closing in on a woman who'd taken shelter in the doorway of the office. Her kneecap exploded in blood and gristle, and she pitched forward. That kept her alive a full two seconds longer, as the second bullet clipped her ear instead of flowering in the centre of her skull.

Two seconds wasn't a lot, but maybe it meant she got to a bonus go-round with her life flashing before her eyes. Frost's third shot finished the job.

Noah and Frost found each other in the middle of the hardstand and took up positions back to back, they had a full three-sixty view of the warehouse between them. They turned in a cautious circle, scanning the shadows and dark spaces for a flicker of movement.

The place was clear.

Eleven corpses.

Lethe stood up, his arms high above his head, "Don't shoot," he called out.

Frost spun around, the dead eye of the Browning pointed straight at Lethe's face.

Noah moved around behind him, double checking his hiding place to be sure there wasn't a nasty surprise waiting to spring out.

"I told you to wait for me. Did I say *anything* about going off and having an adventure of your own? And before you try and argue with me, no I didn't."

Lethe tried to play it cool.

It lasted all of five paces as his rush became a run and he threw his arms around Noah, much to the other man's disgust. Frost was less worried about cool, and just glad to see his man. He scooped Lethe up in huge a bear hug. "The old man was beginning to think you'd defected."

"Better than that, I've been plotting to destroy civilisation."

"Huh?"

"Planting nuclear bombs, my man, no half measures for me."

"Say again?"

"You heard me the first time."

Noah was all business. "Where?"

"One here, the other in Rio. They think it's a new hand for Christ the Redeemer."

"I'll tell Konstantin," Frost said. "Luckily the old man already sent him there, looking for Noah." He engaged his earpiece and moved away.

"Where's the Lima bomb?"

"The Centro Cívico tower. Morais has a remote detonator."

"So we leave the bombs and go for her," Noah said.

"Ideally we neutralise the bombs in case we don't get to her."

"That's when we have twice the amount of firepower."

Frost returned, his line to the old man still open. "The old man wants to know what's going on."

Lethe told them.

When he was finished he asked for a spare mobile. Frost handed him a burner. Lethe took it like it was made of solid gold. "At fucking *last*." He powered it up and launched the browser, navigating directly to Nonesuch. In seconds he established a VPN connection to the manor's servers. He keyed in his password, unlocking the encryption, and finally breathed out as his familiar interface installed itself to the phone, taking over its functionality. Less than a minute later he held what was essentially a remote that steered the complex network of high-powered computers Lethe had designed, built, configured and programmed himself.

He was back in The Nest.

"Think of the roaming charges," Noah said with a grin. "The old man is going to shit a brick when he gets the bill."

"We need to move," Frost said.

"Yes, right. Divide and conquer. Noah, you and I should go after Morais. If we get close enough I can jam her phone with this," he waved the phone, "but I mean *close*."

"We get *that* close, we take her out, we don't fuck about jamming phones," Noah said, bluntly.

"Frost, you need to get to the tower and neutralise the bomb. Do whatever you have to do to make sure that thing doesn't go of if we'd don't find her."

"If I'm getting that close to the bomb, I'm banking on you boys not to let it go off."

"There are three green pins on the device. You'll see them. Switch them out for the red ones. That should neutralise the local trigger at least."

Frost looked at the van, but two of the tyres had been blown out in the gunfight.

He left the warehouse on foot, intending to commandeer a vehicle.

"We're going to need transport too," Lethe said. "Come with me."

Noah followed him.

The mobile was still downloading reams of data. Christ, he missed being connected. He ignored his three and a half thousand unread messages and concentrated on engaging his tracking software. He keyed in Morais's mobile number, which he'd committed to memory before he'd even flown out of the UK. He had a good head for numbers. Neurotically so.

"There she is," he said, a devious smile curling at his lips. "No escape now, Prof. We've got eyes on everywhere she goes, we can track her on this."

"Not we," said Noah. "Me. You need to drive."

Lethe stopped dead. "What?"

"Mate, my arms are absolutely wrecked," Noah explained. "They've been chained above my head for three or four days. You really don't want me driving. I can't feel a thing."

"I... I can't."

"Of course you can. You have a license. It's a car. Or it will be when we've stolen one."

"No, I mean I can't drive in this place. It's insane. You've seen it out there."

"Yes you can. And do you know why? Because you *have* to. Simple as that."

Lethe swallowed. Noah was right.

Lethe nodded firmly.

"Good man. Let's go."

He didn't want to think about it.

Down the street, no more than fifty metres away, they saw a man pacing and yelling into a mobile phone. Sweat stains made his shirt cling to his back. He didn't look happy. But then, Frost was driving off in his car, so he had good reason to be pissed off.

Noah ignored him and instead raced over the road, gun still out and pointed low, his arms awkward and stiff by his sides.

A second man across the street was working under the hood of an original VW Beetle.

Noah approached him, but then changed his mind.

Lethe caught up with him as he headed off down a side street opposite the warehouse.

A whole line-up of parked cars queued outside the repair shop in various states of distress ranging from derelict to the bricked-up junker at the far end of the line. The mechanic stood beside a good-looking woman in a pretty yellow sun dress. They were next to a Hyundai Elantra, neither the newest or the oldest car on the street. It looked like it had been built this century and might actually run.

The couple's attention was on the man who'd had his car stolen.

They didn't even acknowledge Noah until he was right up close to them.

"I'm really sorry about this," Lethe said.

"Shut up," Noah cut him off. "Just give me the keys."

The woman saw the gun and screamed. The man stepped forward, gallant, a spanner in his hand, but Noah raised the weapon as high as he could—which meant it was aimed square at the man's cock. That stopped him dead. He stepped back, talking rapidly in Spanish.

"The keys. What the fuck is 'keys' in Spanish?"

"Las llaves?" the man asked, understanding.

"Si, those," snapped Noah. The man fished the keys from his pocket, staring all the while at the gun aimed between his legs.

He held them out to Noah.

Noah indicated the man should give them to Lethe, who fumbled them nervously as he took them, having to scrabble around in the gutter to get them.

Lethe climbed behind the wheel while Noah painfully squeezed himself into the passenger seat. "Here goes nothing." Lethe jammed the key into the ignition and turned it, firing up the engine. He threw the gear into reverse and they screeched out of the parking space, smashing the back bumper into the abandoned shell of a 60's Camaro. The woman hurled a volley of invective at his back. Lethe ignored her and pulled away.

"Follow her on the phone, tell me exactly where she's going. We've got to catch up with her before she's seven miles clear of the tower. That's the blast radius."

"Comforting," Noah said.

He sat with the mobile in his lap, his hands shaking violently as he tried to move the map around on the screen. Twice he almost dropped the phone.

Lethe eyed him with concern, wondering how the hell this was going to go down.

On the bright side, if he wrecked the car it wouldn't screw with his no-claims bonus.

THIRTY SIX

Frost tapped the steering wheel of the stolen Buick in frustration.

The car was overly large, with vague steering and ridiculously soft suspension.

Carjackers couldn't be choosers.

The roads around central Lima were gridlocked. The evening rush hour coupled with the bombing at the *Plaza des Armas* had assured no one was getting anywhere fast—unless they drove like Martin.

The satnav wasn't much use. For the fifth time in as many minutes he checked the distance between him and the Centro Civico Tower. It was still far too far away to walk, but sitting here wasn't getting him anywhere. This was technically a three lane road, on which the traffic sat five abreast. Frost couldn't see an end to the tailback. And even if he'd wanted to get out and run, they were so tightly packed in, he would barely be able to open his door more than a few inches.

Frost used his earbud to check in with Konstantin Khavin.

The Russian answered.

"Stop calling me, it's getting embarrassing now."

"I'm getting nowhere fast. You?"

"Final approach to the cable car station. I can see Christ from here. He's... big."

"That he is. He's got a bit of a cult following," Ronan said.

"You're not as funny as Noah," the Russian said. "So stop calling me. I'm not your girlfriend. I will call you know when I have disarmed the weapon. And if I don't succeed, no weepy goodbye. Now leave me alone."

The line went dead. Typical Koni. As last words went, they weren't exactly the best to part on.

The one consolation was the dense traffic delayed Morais too, buying Frost the same time as it was costing him. The traffic gods took away with one hand and gave with another.

Giving up, he pushed his door open, the edge of the metal leaving a dent in his neighbour's car. The driver peeled down his window and hurled a volley of abuse. The gap wasn't wide enough for Frost to squeeze through.

He checked the passenger side, but it wasn't any better.

So instead he opened the sunroof.

He disconnected the satnav and using both hands, levered himself up and climbed out onto the roof. The dizzying heat was down to the mid 20s. He ignored the cacophony of horns and jumped down from the bonnet onto the boot of the next car ahead, a much smaller green Fiat. There was nowhere on the road to actually put his feet, so from there he jumped to his left, straddling two vehicles, his front foot landing on the back of a rusty old pickup. He clambered up onto the cab.

The driver stuck his head out of the side window, cursing him out.

Frost surveyed the ocean of cars ahead.

The only vehicles moving were motorbikes and mopeds, and they were weaving dangerously between the stationary cars and trucks, making use of every inch of space to squeeze their way through.

He'd always preferred bikes over cars, anyway.

He jumped from car to car, taking the fastest route possible from where he was to the side of the road and planted down both feet on the narrow pavement. He barged his way through the tourists, peddlers, businessmen and tramps.

He saw a teenager on a moped moving slowly up ahead. He was waiting for a gap in the flow, and then driving up onto the pavement for a few metres before dropping back to the road and crawling along the gutter.

Frost wasn't about to risk it all on a moped. He scanned the crowds for another bike, something with a bit of horsepower to it. He saw a helmetless woman riding an Indian Super Scout 249. The bike was over sixty-five years old, but it purred like a brand new Harley.

Frost drew his Browning.

The woman tried to steer past him, her eyes filled with panic.

Frost had no intention of firing, but for some reason he'd figured she'd stop. She didn't, she veered around him, causing Frost to kick out, pitching the woman from the saddle. She crashed into a postcard stand. Frost let her fall, making a grab for the bike.

A shopper crouched down beside the fallen woman. Frost left them to it. He didn't have time to worry about hurt feelings and a few bruises. He gunned the engine and steered along the pavement. People leapt from his path before they were mown down. He was only going twenty, but on the busy walkway it was more like seventy and potentially lethal.

Frost was on edge; veering left and right, gunning the engine as a warning to those up ahead.

He glanced down at the satnav and turned sharply to the right, almost careening into an elderly woman struggling with bulging string shopping bags spilled to overflowing with fresh vegetables. A greasy haired guy in a football shirt chased him down, trying to knock him off and end his crazy warpath. Frost rolled with the attempted blow, ducked and slammed his elbow into his pursuer's face, hard, causing blood to explode from his ruptured nose.

Emboldened by the courage of the do-gooder, others took up his mantle, running to mount their own bikes and give chase.

Meaning Frost had to lose them all now.

He turned into a side road, ducking under lines of laundry, and weaving across a small square of paving slabs that funnelled down into a much narrower alley. His first thought was that he'd driven himself into a dead end. It was so much quieter here. Frost gunned the engine and hurtled towards the mouth of the narrower avenue, racing the angry mob trying to cut off his escape.

He was approaching the mouth of the alley fast, but he didn't slow down. At the last moment, when it was too late to pull out, he realised the ground dropped away beneath him in a flight of steps. He hit them fast, standing on his feet for the juddering descent, his knees absorbing the brutal impact.

At the bottom, he stopped and glanced back.

The angry locals reached the top of the steps, but those on bikes were reluctant to follow.

He was way out in front now. He knew it and they knew it.

He had the luxury of time to glance down at the satnav and get his bearings before he roared off along the quiet backstreet.

THIRTY SEVEN

Lethe forced himself to breathe.

Every car on the road was too close. A microbus in front of him crawled along, continually cutting across his path. It kept weaving back and forth, trying to find space to pick up speed between picking up people. The cramped camper vans ignored formal bus stops and pulled up wherever they fancied. And all the while it sounded its alarm, a strung-together medley of annoying horn sounds, like a siren calling out for fares so they'd know it was coming.

The next time it abruptly halted, Lethe put his foot down, aiming for a gap to ghost around it, only to slam on the brakes a split second later as a battered Ford Escort forty years old if it was a day, surged into the space vacated by the bus.

"You've got to be more aggressive, Jude."

In response, Lethe wrenched the wheel to one side, the front bumper of the Hyundai ramming into a beige 80's Mercedes. Lethe dragged the bumper along the side his victim, mounting the kerb to squeeze past the Merc and its irate driver. He cut sharply through a gap that he forced open in the traffic.

"More like it. Next left," Noah yelled, glancing up from his mobile phone.

The next left was a few feet ahead of them; Lethe turned so hard he thought the car would pitch over. More horns brayed at the move. It was a game the drivers liked to play. They raced down a quieter street, with a park on one side and a concrete wall daubed with inventive graffiti on the other, most of it political commentary with the names and likenesses of candidates. Lethe took advantage of the quieter road to floor the accelerator. The little car wasn't exactly a Ferrari, but it got the job done.

Lethe didn't slow as he approached a crossroads.

He gritted his teeth, hit the horn, and drove straight through it.

He didn't look, and somehow they didn't die.

"We're going to have to rejoin the main road."

"Oh joy," said Lethe.

"Okay, left here."

The entered a slip road that took them back to a major street. They were far enough away from the centre now that the traffic was at least moving, but that didn't change how insanely busy it was.

"Just force your way in," Noah said.

Easier said than done when the car you were trying to bully out of the way was a huge lorry.

He fought the instinct to brake hard and instead punched the accelerator and ploughed on instead, forcing the big rig to brake hard. Its brakes locked up, and for one sickening moment the back end swung out sliding across into the next lane. Lethe didn't slow down. He forced another twenty miles per hour out of the engine, veering into the next lane to fill a gap that, right at that moment was only marginally smaller than his car. He couldn't stop. He was committed to the move.

He couldn't worry about the truck; that was the truck driver's responsibility.

A driver with a death wish fought him for the gap. Lethe chickened out at the last second and slammed on the brakes before they collided. Instead of sparing them the wreck, they were rear-ended.

Noah and Lethe pitched forward and were thrown back into their seats.

It took a moment to realise what had just happened. In that time the driver who'd rammed them got out of his car.

"Just go!" Noah yelled. Lethe didn't need telling. He restarted the stalled engine, shoved the car into gear and drove away, forcing his way into another lane. With a crunch he sideswiped the front wing of another vehicle. And then clipped the wing mirror off the next.

"Always forward," Noah said.

Lethe followed his direction. He kept gassing it. They passed a line of shops that had died out a decade ago back home, a shoe shine place, a record store, a social club whose tables had spilled out into the street, and a hole in the wall coffee bar. The car lurched forward, forcing another microbus to swerve out of the way as it foolishly tried to occupy the same space in front of them.

It was chaos now.

A chain reaction of collisions trailed in the Hyundai's wake.

Cars moving at speed, packed close together, had no time to react as a succession of vehicles spun out into their path.

Lethe's heart raced as he barely avoided another car in his way. He needed to put as much distance between him and the pile up as possible, and that meant taking more risks, not fewer.

"Next right. Thirty feet."

Lethe didn't need telling twice.

He wrenched the wheel over, not touching the brake.

The Hyundai launched into the far right lane, cutting up a grocery flatbed truck.

Lethe steered down the side street. The horns were ever-present now. Not all of them were down to his defensive driving.

"This'll take us out to the highway. Morais is out of town, on the highway already. Got about half a mile until she's out of the blast zone."

Lethe pushed harder on the accelerator, even though it wouldn't go any further. They gained momentum, speeding up the cloverleaf and onto the highway. It was busy, but unlike the city behind them, not bumper-to-bumper.

The density of buildings and population noticeably reduced over the next quarter mile. When Lethe glanced to his left he saw one of the many mountains surrounding the city, dry and dusty and bleached of any greenery. The lower half of the rocky face, where the incline was at its least steep, was densely packed with row upon row of tenement housing that haphazardly came together to form rough streets. There wasn't a single power line or street light.

The houses were a riot of bright colours, painted to try to distract from the sheer hopelessness of the ghetto. No amount of emulsion was going to paint over the poverty, but they were the most colourful slums Lethe had ever seen. There were no paved roads, no gardens and no public squares, none of the usual elements of urban life. Just dust and broken stones and brightly coloured walls.

Lethe returned his attention to the road. They may be dirt poor, put none of them deserved what was coming to them.

They had to stop it.

"Distance?"

"Not close enough."

"Turn on the jammer anyway."

"Going to check in with old man first," Noah dialled a number and with some difficulty, held the phone to his ear. Lethe could only hear Noah's side of the conversation. It was enough.

"It's me. Yep, we're closing in on Morais. Frosty's on his way to the Lima bomb. Any word from Koni? The military? Lucky bastard. How come we're on our own and he gets all the help? What about the fucking Peruvian military? Oh really? Why am I not surprised? Okay then, I guess we're on our own. Jude's rigged up this single dampener so we'll be out of contact for a while. And if we can actually get close enough, you won't be able to reach Morais either. Put it this way, if you can call her, we're fucked," Noah listened for a few seconds. "Sorry, boss, no way. Can't guarantee she's coming out of this alive. Not our priority. This is about the bomb. Nothing else matters. No. I said no." Noah hung up the phone and started typing a text message. Lethe wasn't used to hearing anyone say no to the old man. What he couldn't understand, assuming he'd pieced the conversation together correctly, was why the old man was insisting on Morais's safety. It didn't make sense, given the stakes.

"Rio's under control," Noah said.

"Good old Koni. And we're on our own?"

"You know it, baby. Wouldn't have it any other way."

Lethe was already going forty over the speed limit, and accelerating. The distance between them and Morais had to close.

Up ahead, with half a dozen cars between them, Lethe caught a glimpse of the Impreza's rear bumper.

He narrowed the gap to five cars.

THIRTY EIGHT

Frost tapped his ear bud as he worked on the service entrance lock at the rear of the building.

"What's the word?"

"We've got eyes on the Prof," Noah replied. "How's it going your end?"

"There's a door between me and where I want to be."

"Jude placed the device on the top floor, in a vacant office suite. The good news is there's an elevator."

"And the bad?"

"He neutralised it so it won't go all the way to the top."

"Ten floors?"

"Roger that. Go do your thing, Frosty. We're going off radar until this is over."

He didn't say good luck. They didn't do stuff like that. There was no such thing, as far as he was concerned. The world was governed by skill, by knowledge, and by manipulation of both those two variables combined.

Frost killed the call as the door sprang open.

His fumbling triggered the alarm, but the reality was a little ringing in his ears was inconsequential. He could handle security, even if he'd rather not.

He slipped inside.

The place was empty. Eerily so, but it was after the end of the work day. Back home, this place would have been filled with people trying to get ahead until late into the night, even if they were just the long distance commuters who chose to stay late to avoid travelling during rush hour. He checked his watch. Cleaners were a bigger issue at a time like this. Without Lethe in his ear talking him through the security and movements of the hot spots inside the building he was blind. He quite liked that. Mind you, given a choice between streaming music and vinyl he was a vinyl-every-time kind of guy, so some psyche profile would probably say he had a yearning to live in a simpler time or some such BS.

Frost proceeded cautiously, but still moving at pace through the lower corridors. He could hear movement in there, so knew he wasn't alone. He flattened himself up against a wall as an internal door whispered open, the brushes that trapped the air-conditioned air in the only giveaway that the door had opened. That forewarning saved the security guard's life. The man, overweight and scruffy, came shambling along the corridor in the direction of the break room, which just so happened to be the direction of the service entrance. He was armed, which wasn't ideal. Frost didn't have time for pleasantries. As the guard approached, he launched himself forward. There was a moment's dumbfoundment where the fat man looked at him but didn't understand what he was seeing, and by the time his brain registered the fact that Frost was a threat it was too late; a sharp blow to the throat dropped him to the floor. He crumpled soundlessly, slumped up against the wall, clutching his neck as he tried to breathe.

Frost said nothing.

He hurried to the lift and pressed the button, even though it wouldn't take him all the way, it would save nine out of ten flights of stairs and precious seconds in the process.

When the service elevator reached as high as Lethe had reprogrammed it to go he swapped it for the service stairs. The stairwell was cold concrete steps with a steel railing and bare breeze block walls that hadn't been painted. He ran up them, and burst out through a set of double fire doors. Most of the area was open office space, though there were a set of offices over towards the far end. The sun had begun to set redly in the huge panorama windows, casting a blinding light across more than half of the room.

He eyed several security cameras.

He drew his Browning. He always felt better when it was in his hand.

He could smell cigarette smoke.

He wasn't alone. The realisation came a fraction of a second before a flicker of movement to his right caught in his peripheral vision.

Frost ducked into a cubicle, and hunkered down. It was impossible to avoid crinkling the plastic coverings that had been draped over everything. He edged forward, just far enough that he could see a figure stepping out through the door of the empty suite at the far end of the open office area. The man had no idea he was there. That would change, but only when Frost wanted it to.

Frost broke cover, moving from cubicle to cubicle to get closer to the Shining Path's man. That meant sacrificing his view of the fire doors and the elevator; but he had other senses. He'd just have to rely on them to make sure he wasn't caught off guard.

He heard more movement.

At least two people were inside the empty suite. He saw their shadows through the glass, despite the blinding reflection filled with Shepherd's delight. He had to assume they were armed and dangerous, which as Noah liked to say just made things more interesting.

He slowed his breathing.

He checked the Browning, making sure he had the shots left, then stood up and walked calmly towards the office. It was all about belonging. Pull that off, make it look like he'd been sent by Morais, and the element of surprise was his. Across to his right, in the heat of the window, he saw a large crate. The two terrorists were guarding it. One man, one woman.

During the few seconds it took to walk up to them, Frost carried out a threat assessment on the pair of them, working out which one he needed to kill first. The woman had corded muscles, and abs that in another place and time would have weakened his knees. There was a tattoo on her bicep that marked her as Revolutionary Armed Forces, a survivor of conflicts in Venezuela, Columbia and Bolivia. The specific design placed her in Santa Cruz during the Pact of Casanare, which meant she'd served as paramilitary during the rigged election. Lego soldiers like her often showed off who they'd killed and cheated on their bodies as a way of keeping score. And she'd amassed a decent tally. She was a survivor.

He shot her first.

He walked relentlessly forward pulling the trigger three times in rapid succession, tearing out her throat. There was no subtly to it. She didn't get a shot off. So maybe she wasn't a survivor after all.

Her partner panicked.

He let rip with his AK-47 indiscriminately, unloading the full clip in the direction of the door, but Frost was already at the window, using the bomb crate as cover.

By the time the man realised where Frost was, he was already dead.

Frost walked over to the two corpses. He relieved the man of his weapon. The headshot had killed him instantly. The woman was dead, but her brain hadn't caught up with the reality of her situation. She clutched at her neck vainly to stop her life pumping out between her fingers. He kicked her weapon away and stood over her, watching her die. It only took a couple of seconds, and in that time she stared at him with such pure hatred it kept the light burning longer than it had any right to. But even rage couldn't keep her alive with the carotid ruptured.

Mission almost accomplished, thought Frost.

The rest was down to Konstantin in Rio and Lethe and Noah across town.

THIRTY NINE

"Stay on her!"

Lethe drove the Hyundai like a man possessed; tailgating the Impreza.

He didn't have the luxury of distance, his makeshift jammer only worked close up, so if she managed to put even a little distance between them she'd be able to detonate the devices, and that didn't bear contemplating.

Noah had his hands on the dashboard and was stretching his back and his shoulders as best he could while still strapped into his seat. He gripped and released the plastic fittings over and over, working his fingers.

In front of them, Morais swerved around a motorbike.

Lethe was forced in behind it.

That bought Morais a chance. She accelerated.

The Impreza was right on the edge of the mobile jammer's range.

Lethe gripped the wheel still tighter. He couldn't see any obvious options.

Two lorries boxed him in on either side.

There was no other option.

He pushed his foot flat to the floor, accelerating into the motorbike's rear wheel.

He couldn't worry about the biker as he went up over the top of their car, bouncing away like a discarded rag doll to lie motionless on the road behind them. The bike's back end swung around and fell, cannoning off their radiator grille and spinning away beneath the lorry beside them. In his mirror, Lethe saw the car behind them run over the stricken rider, ending whatever chances he had left. The guy hadn't been wearing a helmet, but even if he had it wouldn't have saved him.

Lethe closed the distance between himself and Morais, bringing her back into range.

"Don't think about it," Noah said, reading his mind. "You did what you had to."

"I killed him."

"Yes. You did. But in doing so you most likely saved everyone he has ever loved. He'd have paid that price willingly if you'd asked him," Noah rationalised.

All he knew was that Morais was more than capable of pushing the button.

He saw Romero lean out of the car ahead of them, head and shoulders through the passenger window. He had an assault rifle in his hands. He couldn't aim properly, but he could make life difficult for them as he squeezed off one shot, then another. Lethe was doing over a hundred, swerving in and out of traffic as he chased Morais. Both shots whistled well wide of the mark, but Lethe ducked instinctively with each report.

"Stay calm," said Noah. "He's not going to hit you. Just focus on doing what you're doing. Let him waste his bullets." It sounded reasonable, even as Romero fired again. This time his aim went so far wide of the mark it hit the driver in the car beside them. The vehicle immediately jerked to its left, grinding up against the car in the next lane, starting a chain reaction. A lorry collided with that car, and so it went.

Lethe was already ahead of the carnage.

He didn't look in his mirror this time. He didn't want to know what was happening behind him.

He matched Morais in every lane shift and speed change, keeping as much distance between them as he dared, zigzagging constantly in the confined space in an attempt to thwart Romero's marksmanship as best as he could.

Police sirens sounded in the distance.

Lethe pushed the small car as hard as he could. It was newer than the Impreza, but the engine was smaller, but the reality was that the only reason they were keeping up was because other vehicles kept slowing Morais down. Twenty metres was nothing. And with traffic thinning out as they went further out of town, the inevitability of her pulling away beyond the range of his signal damper became acute.

"We need to finish this," he said.

But Noah couldn't hear him over the rush of air as he opened his window. He was thinking the same way. With his left hand, he gestured at Lethe to move over into the left lane. With his right, he held his gun out of the window.

His grip was stronger than it had been, even so Lethe prayed Noah could hold on to it against the relentless battering of the aerodynamic tunnel the car was carving out.

Noah did better than that.

He fired three unsteady shots.

They went wide.

One hit a truck tire, but they were built to withstand blowouts. The rubber quickly shredded, peeling away to bounce across the highway into the wall.

Noah didn't waver. He stared dead ahead, eyes on the Impreza.

And kept on shooting.

"Big picture," Lethe said, the blistering rage of wind stealing away his words without providing any comfort.

Something leaked from underneath the Impreza. He saw a trail of black begin to form.

There was no glorious Hollywood-style explosion, but if Noah had hit the petrol line they were going to come to a sticky end sooner rather than later.

Much sooner.

Suddenly, the Impreza swerved *hard* to the right, cutting across three lanes of traffic. The suicidal manoeuvre caused several cars to lock up their brakes as they tried to avoid being side-swiped and bullied off the road.

Morais was hell bent on reaching the next off ramp.

He couldn't wait for Noah to get his head back inside the car; he had to follow.

The Hyundai screeched into the next lane, barely squeezing in behind another car making its way over to the exit. Noah whipped his head back inside as they came perilously close to the side of an original Camero running parallel to them in the next lane. Morais was ahead and to the right of the Camero, still changing lanes.

Lethe had no choice but to follow.

He edged slightly ahead of the Camero, there wasn't room for him to get over, but he was going over anyway. Lethe steered hard right, ramming it with the Hyundai's rear wing. He kept his foot down, pushing both cars to the edge of the road. The other driver fought him, wheels locked, only to spin out.

The impact lost Lethe precious speed.

Noah fired twice through the open window.

224

The noise inside the cabin was deafening.

One of the bullets struck its mark.

The Impreza's rear tire blew out and the car spun.

Lethe accelerated towards the spinning Impreza, his only thought to ram it.

The front wing of the Hyundai smashed into the back of the Impreza as Morais wrestled with the wheel, sending the other car spinning in the opposite direction. The impact threw Noah and Lethe forward in their seats.

There was a gunpowder crack of an explosion as the airbags deployed, nearly taking Lethe's thumbs off.

The Hyundai stopped spinning.

Lethe couldn't move from the shock of the impact, pinned into his seat by the airbag. It felt like he'd been punched in the chest by a bastard holding a brick.

He was frozen.

His limbs wouldn't obey him.

Everything was dazed and distant, vague, like watching everything play out from somewhere far away.

Noah on the other hand, was out of the car in a second, door flung wide and striding towards the Impreza, firing his gun once with every step until he emptied the clip.

He reloaded five steps away from the other car.

The gunshots woke Lethe up.

The airbag had begun to slowly deflate. He pushed at it, trying to force the air out of it faster, then released his seat belt. The mobile phone was on the floor where Noah had dropped it.

Despite his spinning head, Lethe managed to reach down and fumble for it. With the phone in his hand he opened his door and fell out onto the tarmac.

Other cars thundered by.

He heard the crack of Romero firing his rifle at Noah, and saw that the other man was out of his car and laying down fire to pin Noah down beside the open passenger door. Worse, Morais was running in the other direction and she was nearly out of range. Without thinking, Lethe pushed himself to his feet and took off sprinting after her.

Immediately, Romero shifted his focus and took a wild shot at Lethe. It was the mistake that cost the general his life. Noah emerged from behind the open door, and planted two bullets in Romero's chest.

Two bullets ended half of a revolution.

The general went down without firing another shot.

Lethe sprinted after Morais, arms and legs pumping furiously as he desperately tried to catch up, but she was so much fitter than him. All he had was the adrenaline and anger burning away in the furnace of his gut to drive him—and that promise he'd made to everyone who had died because of him along the way.

She had to pay for what she'd done; to Cathy, to Beatriz, to the tourists on the train, to the biker he'd hit so he could catch her in time, to all of them.

She had to die before she could detonate the bomb.

She ran down the embankment, skidding and sliding and pushed herself back up to her feet, and carried on running out into the middle of a dusty field. Beyond her loomed the mountains, and at their base, more tenements. She kept on running.

He saw her clutching her phone, stabbing uselessly at it as she ran, but as long as he kept close it wasn't going to respond to any amount of taps. If she concentrated on just running he'd never catch her. His lungs were bursting, every laboured gasp burned as he sucked it down, and his legs were like jelly, the muscles ready to give out, but still he chased her.

Morais stopped dead in her tracks and turned to face him. She was smiling.

He saw her reach down to draw her own gun, and realised he'd fucked up. Again.

She had not been trying to escape, she'd been putting distance between them and Noah. Lethe glanced over his shoulder, still straining to breathe. And it had worked. Noah was struggling to close the distance between them. His injuries slowed him down.

His gun was up, but there was no way he was going to fire with Lethe between him and his target.

Lethe turned back to face Camilla Morais.

"I really didn't think you had it in you, Mr Lethe," she said coldly. "I don't like being surprised."

He expected the shot, but it didn't come.

Lethe grasped the dynamics of the standoff. He was no threat to her. He was insurance. While he was alive, Noah wouldn't shoot. But as soon as Noah was in range she'd take the shot, kill him and turn her gun on Lethe. It was about the order of the threat. Noah was a predator, he wasn't. He was prey.

"Drop your gun or I end your friend's life," Morais called, her words carrying back to Noah despite the roar of traffic back on the highway.

He carried on running across the scrubland.

"You really don't get it, do you?" Noah yelled back, stilling running, his gun raised as high as his arm would allow. "If it's him or millions of people, Judy dies every time."

Morais fired two shots and Noah pitched forward into the dirt.

Lethe stared in horror. He couldn't focus. He couldn't think. It was impossible. It didn't end like this. It couldn't. He screamed, but there were no words.

Morais swung the gun back to cover him. "I don't want to kill you unless I have to. Turn off the jammer."

Inside his head, Lethe screamed fuck you. In the field, Lethe said nothing.

"Do the smart thing, Jude. Once you're dead I can just walk away. Your little toy won't save anyone."

He finally found the words. "Shoot me," he said. Not loudly, not defiantly.

"If you insist," she said. But she didn't pull the trigger. She walked away from him as though he was irrelevant. He took one step then another and another, following her. Keeping her within the dampening field of the phone's jamming effect.

She turned after fifteen steps.

"I can still use you, Jude," she said. "There's still a place for you in the new world now Romero's dead. He was the figurehead. The rallying point. He was the reason for people to follow us. He was the one they'd look to when the fallout settled. I don't know if I can do this without him. But you, you can replace him. With your gifts you can create a legend we can all look to. An ideal we can aspire to. You have it in your hands to change the world. To make it a better place."

"Put down the gun," he said, sounding more confident than he felt.

She shook her head. "I've worked too hard, sacrificed too much. This is a once in a lifetime chance to effect change. Now, enough of this nonsense. Do as you're told, turn off the jammer."

Morais had walked them around in a wide circle now and she was backing towards where Noah had fallen.

Still Morais retreated, and still Lethe followed her.

He glanced at his mobile. It was dead. Sometime over the last couple of minutes the juice had run out, the charge the signal dampener demanded burning through the small battery far quicker than he'd expected. Lethe couldn't risk staring at the device and couldn't allow the abject gut-wrenching twist of terror he felt to register on his face.

Which meant that Morais's mobile was no longer jammed. All she had to do was press the button once and it was all over. She kept her eyes fixed on him, her gun trained on his head.

Lethe tried to think of a way to distract her. He couldn't let her look at her phone...

And then it rang, shattering the moment.

She didn't understand. She stared down at the phone in her hand, still walking backwards, trying to work it out.

The ring tone persisted, demanding to be answered. She stared at the screen. He had no idea how far they'd run—or if they were still within the blast zone. It had to be close. They were right on the fringe, maybe not vaporised immediately, but battered by the nuclear winds, and sickened by the fallout.

Did Morais realise that?

Still the phone rang.

Still she stared at it.

"I'll let you say goodbye," she said, finally answering the call on speaker. She didn't take her eyes off Lethe. "You'll have to speak up," she said. "It's pretty noisy out here, Charles."

"Camila? I've been trying to reach you."

"Why? To say goodbye? To get all mawkish and sentimental after all this time?"

"Have you detonated the bomb?"

"Not yet."

"Good. That's very good. Let me help you. Please. I want to help you."

"You want to help me?"

"Yes, of course. You may hate me, but that doesn't mean I hate you. I never have, Camila. I love you. I always have and I always will."

"You're lying."

"I'm too old for lies, my dear."

"I loved you once," Morais said, she was crying now. "But then I grew up. I'm sorry, Charles."

"You didn't always call me that."

"No. But that was just another lie, wasn't it, *father*."

Lethe's eyes widened.

"Not a lie," the old man's voice was thin and reedy through the speaker. "You'll always be my little girl, no matter what you think. The day I rescued you from that terrible orphanage was the single most important day of my life. I would do *anything* for you. Even this."

Morais raised her gun towards Lethe.

"I'm going to shoot Jude now. Larkin is already dead."

"Please, Camila. Please don't do this. He's like you. He's your brother. We are the closest thing you have to a real family."

She shook her head. "I've never had a family. Say goodbye to your 'son'."

Lethe saw her take aim. He watched her steady her hand. She couldn't miss from this range. He closed his eyes.

A single gunshot rang out.

FORTY

But he didn't die.

Morais was on the ground, blood staining the dirt beneath her head.

Behind her, Noah was sprawled on the ground on his side. He held his gun in both hands, braced to steady the shot, still aiming in case she got up again, and gritting his teeth against the pain.

Lethe dropped to his knees, all the fight draining from him.

Sir Charles's voice could still be heard from Morais's mobile phone.

"Camila? Are you there? Camila? Jude! Oh God, girl, what did you *do*?"

FORTY ONE

They waited for Frost.

He arrived on a stolen motorbike.

Lethe was in cuffs, the police trying to question him, but he kept reading the same *no comprende* denial over and over. Frost focussed on Noah. Paramedics had been working on him for half an hour. He could hear him berating the medics, which was a good sign, but there was only so much abuse any one man could take, and over the last few days Noah Larkin had taken a damned sight more than that threshold.

Frost parked up and walked over to the police cordon which had been set up in a wide circle in the middle of the dusty field, marking off the two crashed cars and the bodies of Morais and the general. The Irishman regarded Morais's corpse for a moment and then approached Lethe.

The officer saw him approach. Frost told her, "This is my scene now," and flashed his ID. She tried to argue, right up until the words "Diplomatic immunity" came out of his mouth, then she regarded Lethe like dirt, but she took the cuffs off as she spat onto the ground. It was a lie. None of them had any such diplomatic protection. Everything they did was off the books. They were on their own out here. The local law enforcement backed off. She'd be back, but for now she simply assumed those magic words actually mattered worth a damn.

Frost squeezed Lethe's shoulder reassuringly for a moment.

"Did you...?" Lethe asked.

Frost nodded. "All sorted, and the old man liaised with local forces to make sure it's being taken care of. You're a hero, matey. This, all of it, is down to you."

"Hardly."

"Don't sell yourself short. Without you, you know what would have happened if you hadn't thought and acted on your feet. You did good."

"I helped plant the bombs," Lethe objected.

"And you stopped them from going off, which is more points in the hero column than the villain column in my book. Look, there's no getting around it, this is going to screw you up. You killed people. That changes you. It just does. Don't take this the wrong way, but I think we should find you someone to talk to when we get back to Nonesuch."

"A shrink?" Lethe shook his head. "I'm fine."

"You're not. You're desensitised. That's different. Remember I've been where you are. It's going to come crashing down on you soon enough. I'm not going to let you get crushed beneath it. Okay? Promise me you'll talk to someone."

"Fine, I promise," Lethe muttered. He knew the statistics on PTSD in war veterans, and those guys were trained for combat. It was all too easy to dismiss, but like it or not, Frost was right. He changed the subject.

"I suppose Peru is a paid up member of the Nuclear Club now."

"Not for long. The old man's called in the IAEA. There'll be a shitload of pressure from on high until the government hand them over. Speaking of, how many are we talking about?"

"Four. The two we've neutralised here, two more."

"Where are they?"

Lethe gave a wry smile. "No idea, but give me a laptop and ten minutes and I can find them for you."

"And there's the Jude Lethe I know and love. You do your thing, I'll go check on Noah." As he turned to walk away Lethe said:

"Ronan?"

The Irishman stopped and turned back.

"Yep?"

"Thank you."

"No need. It's what we do."

"Can I ask you a favour?"

"Name it."

"When we get back to Nonesuch, will you teach me some moves?"

"What sort of moves?"

"You know, how to fight, how to fire a gun without actually shooting myself in the foot. And maybe how to withstand torture."

Frost looked at his friend, thinking about it. "That's not the kind of stuff you learn overnight, Jude. And to be honest I'm not sure you ever really want to learn it. It's not good for your soul. And you've still got a basically good soul."

"Just the basics."

"Are you planning on more excursions now you've got a taste for fast living?"

"Fuck no. Just for peace of mind. I felt so helpless out here." Lethe raised a hand to scratch his nose. He stopped before his fingers touched his face.

His hand was shaking.

Frost saw, and understood.

"Okay, now's as good a time as any to let you into the secret life of us. First lesson, just because you helped save the world don't expect a medal."

"I never expected one."

"Excellent. See you've learned something already. That's today's lesson complete. Tomorrow's begins when we get home."

Frost saw that the paramedics were struggling trying loading Noah into an ambulance. Noah smiled at Frost as he approached.

"Not dead then?"

"Not yet."

"Good. I get the feeling life would be pretty boring without you around."

"Ah, man, don't make me go all mushy on you."

"Wouldn't dream of it. Anyway, get your shit together. The old man wants us back in Poland. Orla's in trouble."

Noah pushed the paramedic away, peeling off the drip they'd fought for so long to insert, and grabbed onto the side of the ambulance's doors with both hands, levering himself up off the stretcher. He was unsteady on his feet. The paramedics berated him in a flurry of words that went by too quickly for Frost to understand.

"Is he going to die?" he asked the nearest medic.

She shook her head, "No, but—"

"That's all I needed to know. Come on, Jude, we're all going home."

The End

THE OGMIOS DIRECTIVE

Crucible
Steven Savile & Steve Lockley

Solomon's Seal
Steven Savile & Steve Lockley

Lucifer's Machine
Steven Savile & Rick Chesler

Wargod
Steven Savile & Sean Ellis

Shining Ones
Steven Savile & Richard Salter

Argo
Steven Savile & Ashley Knight

www.ingramcontent.com/pod-product-compliance
Ingram Content Group UK Ltd.
Pitfield, Milton Keynes, MK11 3LW, UK
UKHW021323180426
11947UKWH00017B/1394